Lucy Helen Muriel Soulsby

Stray thoughts on reading

Lucy Helen Muriel Soulsby

Stray thoughts on reading

ISBN/EAN: 9783337284077

Printed in Europe, USA, Canada, Australia, Japan

Cover: Foto ©Andreas Hilbeck / pixelio.de

More available books at **www.hansebooks.com**

ON

READING

BY

LUCY H. M. SOULSBY

FIFTH IMPRESSION

LONGMANS, GREEN, AND CO.

39 PATERNOSTER ROW, LONDON

NEW YORK AND BOMBAY

1904

PREFACE.

THOSE to whom these papers are dedicated will recognize old friends, and will have a key to the apparently causeless diversity of the subjects dwelt on.

The forbearance of others can only be asked for on the score of the tacit apology conveyed by my title—an apology for both discursiveness of subject and slightness of treatment.

These thoughts, ranging as they do from " Romola " to the " Pilgrim's Progress," will seem "woefully astray" as far as any connection of ideas goes; but if they recall to the reader's mind the books discussed, my deficiencies will be condoned in consideration of the happy memories awakened by these papers.

LUCY H. M. SOULSBY.

THE MANOR HOUSE,
BRONDESBURY PARK,
October, 1897.

CONTENTS.

"If my life had been more full of calamity than it has been, I would live it over again, to have read the books I did in my youth."—W Hazlitt.

"THINGS in books' clothing!" It was thus that one of the most fascinating of all writers spoke of the solid improving books for which I am going to hold a brief.

It would have "moved the spleen" of that most "genuine lover of reading," Charles Lamb, to hear of our Half Hours' Reading Societies, and "Hundred Best Books;"—how would threepenny classics have wounded the feelings of him who found even octavo editions of Beaumont and Fletcher "painful to look at"!

The vagrant fancy of that scholar gypsy rebelled against the "books that no gentleman's library should be without," yet, surely, even he would be pained to see those books discarded—not (as he would have wished) for the sake of "the thrice noble Margaret," or of Raymond Lully—but, for the morbid psychology, and second-rate passion, and vulgar scandals that cover every railway bookstall. In spite of Elia on the one hand, and the railway bookstall on the other, I

B

want you to consider the question of what books it
"becomes a young woman to know."

I do not pretend that you will be *amused* by
these books, but, if you will work at them for a
couple of years, you will become *interested*, which
is far better.   Amusement dies out with the
repetition of the thing which caused it, whereas
interest deepens and widens as you go on.

When De Quincey was a young man he wrote a
private memorandum of what he should aim at in
order to secure a happy life.   In discussing these
"Constituents of Happiness," he says :—

"Nature provides to all men a sufficient supply
of happiness during that time when they have
sufficient intellect to apprehend and ascertain, or
foresight to *secure* to themselves sources of volun-
tary happiness—an involuntary happiness proceed-
ing from an exuberance of animal joy and spirits;
this she withdraws in regular progression with the
advancement of the intellect.   On the decay of
these self-supporting spirits commences the incum-
bency (which rests on every man) to provide for
himself a source of permanent stimulus; and at this
crisis it is that wisdom most fails the souls of men."

As an assistance to this wisdom, I am going to
propose to you a list of books,[1] which you could
easily work through, during your first five years
after leaving school.   If you took up this plan,

[1] See p. 20.

and carried it out, you would be intellectually in a far better position for facing the world, at twenty-two or twenty-three, than most girls of that age.

I am fully alive to the objections that may be fairly brought against giving such definite form to my suggestions. Some say that girls, on leaving school, should be able to shape their own line of study, that otherwise their education has been a failure.

I grant that the girl who on leaving school says to some guide, philosopher, and friend, "Do tell me what to read," is not the highest success of Higher Education. I should admire her more if she had a strong bent and knew exactly what she wanted to do, and scorned stray suggestions; but I have not met this "not impossible she" often enough to feel hampered by her.

I recognize, also, that each one of you has probably some home adviser who could give her a far better list; but I give mine all the same, because I observe that girls sometimes go abroad for confession and direction, when their own mother is fully qualified to meet all their requirements; from which I infer that some of you may adopt my list because it is *not* of home manufacture, and that my having no claim on your allegiance may seem to some of you a reason for your giving it. This same instinct of natural perversity will probably lead others to take exception to my list, because *I* give it. By all means scratch out each name and replace it—only, be sure you read the supplanters. My object will then have been attained. So long as you know the Iliad, I do not care whether you think it the work of Homer, or of another man of the same name. So long as you read, I do not care whether you read my list, or some one else's. Pray do not imagine that I have compiled an official guide to books—I only tell you of those I myself should buy, first and foremost, and should most blush at not knowing. Having told you how far I am from wishing to impose my list as a yoke, I shall not apologize for its personality, as, to my mind, wholly impersonal advice is generally wholly uninteresting.

As I said before, you may very likely find my books dull. If so, do not be rash in expressing your feelings.

Many of these books are accepted by " those who know " as " the precious life-blood of a master spirit,"[1] and it is not for us to presume to award praise or blame. One hears some " unidea'd young lady "[2] announcing that Wordsworth is prosy and Miss Austen dull. I have no doubt she finds them so, but whose fault is that? Do not say a book amuses you when it does not; but, if good judges admire it, try to bring yourself up to its level, and, till you succeed, do not obtrude your

[1] " Areopagitica. "   [2] Dr. Johnson.

own deficiencies. Nothing strikes the note of uncultivation so painfully as the expression of crude judgments.

When you hear people pronouncing on music, or painting, without having studied to inform their judgment and to raise their taste, you are probably struck by a sense of their inadequacy to the occasion, but I suspect you often "rush in" to pass very similar judgment on a *book* that has the misfortune not to appeal to you. Even the invitation of an examination-paper to discuss the merits and demerits of Shakespeare seems to me a direct injury to the moral humility of the examinee : how much more those "literary and social judgments" of private life which have not the same plea of necessity !

Now, suppose that a girl has made her good resolutions about reading, and has chosen her books.

My first advice would be, make easy rules for yourself, and let your time-table be based on the minimum of hours you can count on. If any of you are already embarked in good resolutions, I suspect that to halve what you have imposed on yourself, would produce better results, and would improve your self-respect and home comfort.

I once had a Reading Society with the following rules :—

1. To keep a list of books read.

2. To read half an hour a day (or three hours a week), and to look out all unknown allusions.
3. To read some good poetry daily.
4. To meet once a term, and to bring lists of books read, of unverified quotations, and of unknown allusions.
5. Not to skip.
6. To finish each book.
7. To keep a commonplace-book.
8. To get a Cassell's threepenny classic, once a month and read it.

I think you will admit that these demands were not excessive, and of course half an hour a day is a minimum which will be exceeded by most who care for their subject. But the value lies, not in how many half-hours or how many pages you read, but, in whether or no you read " with both hands and all your teeth." I should be inclined to add to that vigorous old proverb, "and a straight back," for I have no faith in reading that is compatible with an arm-chair. Sit up to the table with note-book and atlas and dictionary at hand ;—write out every unknown quotation or allusion, in a " Hunt Book," for future search.

I was talking the other day to an old lady of eighty-four, who pointed to her books of reference at hand, and said she still kept up her lifelong habit of looking out everything as it came. It cheered one's own outlook on the future to hear her say that at eighty-four she was as keenly interested in every new book and subject, as Athenian to her finger tips, as ever she was in her life. I suspect the vigour and energy which looked out references had something to do with this freshness of mind, and that if we allow ourselves to read at half pressure in youth our faculties will be at half-power long before we are eighty-four.

If possible, make a written abstract of the book, and, in any case, "count your scalps" at the end of the reading hour ;—by which I mean, shut your book and give a clear account to yourself, either verbally or in writing, of what you have learnt. The mathematician who inquired, after reading "Paradise Lost," "What does it prove?" showed an excellent, though somewhat misplaced, habit of mind.

I set great store by the habit of keeping a list of the books read. Arrange it in months, and it will be invaluable as an encouragement to wholesome shame for your shortcomings. It makes your list very interesting in after years, if you enter the place, and the lender, and an expression of opinion about each book.

I should also strongly recommend a common place-book, with an alphabetical index.

While on the subject of direct hints as to how to to read, I should like to suggest that two subjects, at least, should be kept in hand, though very possibly on alternate days or even weeks. Also that one of these should be read with some fulness, so that a group of books on the same subject should be read consecutively.

"Know your centuries," but choose some one century for your special possession.

I read Mrs. Delany's six fat volumes of letters aloud one winter, and followed out the pedigree and fortunes of every one she met—with the result that the number of my personal acquaintances is enlarged by Mrs. Montagu, Mrs. Piozzi, Mrs. Chapone, Miss Burney, the Duchess of Portland, and, in fact, more good company than I have time to name.

I have before me a letter written by a girl of twenty to a girl friend, more than seventy years ago, and I cannot forbear quoting at some length from such an instance of vivid personal interest in historical characters. "So you are reading Gibbon. The style is elegant and the criticism profound, but the philosophy is naught. . . . Poor Ulpian, murdered while covered with his purple, is a shocking story. When you come to Stilicho you will grieve as you read. . . . Belisarius was a great man in the field, but, alas, he was a mean wretch at home ! There is some amazingly fine writing about the death of Julian. The Moslem and Mogul history is very interesting. Most of these gentlemen are domestic acquaintances of mine, and I feel quite inspired whenever I touch Eastern ground. . . . Heroes arise before and after these periods, whom you follow with all your soul : Hannibal and Alexander form a grand contrast of equal powers fighting with, and against, fortune. But were I to choose in the whole world a pedigree, I should derive mine from the great Tancred de Hauteville in Normandy. . . . But I am sure you wish Gibbon at France by this time."

This letter (of which I have not given a tithe) was one of a series of confidential letters written by a girl who thoroughly enjoyed society and all girlish pleasures. I have quoted at this length because it seems to me interesting as a relic of that keen book-hunger which some fear is being improved off the face of the earth by the progress of education, or rather, of instruction.

To return from this digression, if you only read isolated books it will be as though, instead of building a house, you merely collected single bricks. At the same time my list consists mainly of isolated books, because there are so many subjects on which it is important that you should know something to prevent your being a dumb note when they are touched on. But if you have one favourite subject in which you read connectedly, you can keep a relay of isolated books on hand, as your second subject.

For a final caution, I would urge, never think that, for lack of past education, it is useless to try in the present. Begin now : take any book you like, and feel that " here, or nowhere,"[1] is a liberal education. You can begin perfectly well with *no* previous knowledge, *if* you will only look out whatever you come on that is unknown to you. Begin on my list, or any one else's, and I can promise that in three years, though perhaps you may not have a cultivated mind, yet you will have indefinitely increased your power of profiting by the society of those who have. A definite list is cramping to a real reader, but a backbone to others. I should never presume to mention a list to one who could taste the flavour of Elia's " Detached Thoughts on Books and Reading," or of that old-fashioned book, Wilmot's " Pleasures of Literature," but I have many friends who look on reading as a more or less painful duty, and who need help in it.

It is the duty, not the pleasure, of reading that I want to dwell on here,—I do not see how you can honestly try to be good, and yet neglect such a means of grace, such a method of self-discipline, as reading.

I know well that many girls are not always prepared to attempt this duty: they wish heartily for that American institution, " A good time ; " they prefer tennis and chatter to steady reading; they

[1] " Wilheim Meister."

do not offer their life, with its time and talents, as a sacrifice to God—they want it for themselves. Yet there is another side to such a girl: part of her does wish to be on God's side in the great battle of good and evil,—she has " pulses of nobleness and aches of shame." [1] If the Service of God does not yet appeal to her, yet, at moments, the Service of Man fires her enthusiasm :—she is not content to live an altogether empty life, and to feel that the world will be as though she had never been.

We are all—especially girls—very apt to " hide our best selves as we had stolen them," [2] so that I doubt not I have some readers who proclaim that they do not like improving books, that they prefer amusing themselves, and who give a general impression that they " can't be bothered." It is these girls that I am most interested in. I am very happy to come on Real Readers, but they do not need me or any one else, they can swim alone. Real Readers will have done already all I can suggest, and far more too. I want to talk about the necessity of reading when you do *not* enjoy it.

Real Readers will tell you, " it is no use reading as a duty,—do not force yourself,—do not read books ' on principle,' because you are advised so to do,—follow your bent, and, if you have no reading bent, do not invent one, for it will never make you a Real Reader." No, I know it will not,—but

[1] F. W. Myers.   [2] J. R. Lowell.

need this trouble you? Is a Real Reader such a much higher order of being than a girl who cooks, or fiddles, or sketches, or keeps house, or gardens? I myself admire the practical sister quite as much as the bookish one. All the same, I should turn them both on to books, if I had my way,—not for the sake of the information conveyed, but because of the moral qualities acquired by steady reading, which the ordinary girl cannot get so well in any other way. Dr. Johnson said, when Mr. Thrale's brewery was being sold, "Sir, it is not the question of a mere brewery, but of the potentiality of growing rich beyond the dreams of avarice." So it is with reading. It is not the actual book which is in question, but the "potentiality of growing rich" spiritually, as well as mentally.

The Reader by nature will agree at once to the value of this proposed diet, but the Headless Horseman of the family will perhaps object, "Why is it *my* duty to read? Am I not as useful in learning to cut out, or to train the choir, or in managing the garden or the poultry?" Yes, you very possibly accomplish more so, than by plodding through some history, looking at the clock to see when it will be time for conscience to let you go, forgetting what you read yesterday, and devoutly wishing something would prevent you from reading to-morrow. I quite admit you will not become intellectual at that rate, and that you

would have more to show if you had given the
time to your ¡hands, and not to what you are
pleased to call your mind ! But does it matter
what you can *show ?* —is there not something
better, "which weighs not as his work, yet swells
the man's amount " ? [1]

Read that half-hour steadily for one year, and
you will then know that nothing else could have
been such searching self-denial and discipline :—
the very irksomeness of it will have strengthened
your moral fibre in a way no manual drudgery
could have done, for the hardest physical labour
would have been nothing like such a battle with
Sloth. Mental sloth is the besetting sin of most
of us,—we would willingly go through any amount
of routine to save the trouble of thinking, and we
find manual labour (in comparison with mental) to
be soothing syrup for the mind. We live in an
age of much bustle and little contemplation,—of
multiplication of formal prayers, and decrease of
wrestling in prayer,—and we should be very chary
of relaxing any habit which (such as a settled
course of reading) tends to make us sit still and
be thoughtful.

"The power of thinking is a great help in being
spiritual," says Faber, and he puts, next to this,
the habit of reading, which is within the reach of
all,—however it may be with the other gift he

[1] " Rabbi ben Ezra."

speaks of. We must all know cases in which moral strength has been gained by perseverance in this habit. I knew a girl who cared for nothing but yellow-backed novels : she woke up to the fact that she was in a fair way to become an empty-headed frivolous woman. She put her shoulder to the wheel, and worked regularly at books which bored her, and I doubt if now you could find any one who deserves more respect for backbone of character. Mind you, this backbone has been acquired; she had not got it to start with, and, if she had put off reading till her intellect appreciated improving books, she would, to this day, be as weak and self-indulgent as she was originally.

Let me quote again from Faber, in pursuing the question of the moral obligation of reading. " It is very hard," he says, " for one who does not care for reading, to talk without sinning." This speaks for itself, so, I will pass on to another kind of talk, in connection with which we are not always sufficiently alive to our moral responsibilities and need of mental training—I mean, Castle-building. " Every man," says Pascal, " is coloured in time by what is said constantly to him. If you perpetually tell any one he is a fool, he comes at last to believe it. So also with the *interior conversations* which each holds with himself—we are responsible for the way in which they colour our minds." How much vanity and egoism, or resentment and suspicion, are fed by these " interior conversations," which are such a ready weapon for the seven evil spirits who attack minds that are left empty?

S. Hugh urges all to cultivate a love of reading as the only remedy for illness and sorrow; I would add to those evils, the inevitable dulness of life. The gayest, busiest girl is not safe in the future, from passing through long grey stretches of actual loneliness, or of the worse loneliness of depression, and she will be very grateful then to early habits which will enable her to find in books " fast sailing ships to waft her away from present troubles to the Fortunate Isles." [1]

How many girls live in the country and pine because they are in such a bad neighbourhood; yet Dante's Castle of Human Wisdom is within easy reach of them;—whatever their county, Utopia and Arcadia are within its limits;—the Forest of Phantastes lies hard by, where they may meet the Gentle Lady and Heavenly Una. Or, if they ask for more human society, I cannot pity those who can " listen to the flapping of the flame" at a Cranford tea-party, and, when they grumble about their Merrytown, I shall quite sympathize with any offended Mrs. Bennet who assures them "there is quite as much of *that* going on in the country as in town." [2]

Very likely one of these sufferers marries and

[1] J. R. Lowell.   [2] " Pride and Prejudice."

thinks that now the monotony of life is at an end. Not at all. Its possibilities are to a certain extent at an end; no fairy prince can now ride by unexpectedly and carry her off to his kingdom. Very likely her husband (who is not a fairy prince) will be out all day, and she will have nothing to do but to miss her sisters and girl friends, and to brood over every suspicion that her doll is stuffed with sawdust. She rouses herself from this to go to the circulating library, and returns with a re-arrangement of the plot of yesterday's novel. Dante's sinners, who ran their ceaseless round over burning sand, had hardly a worse lot than one who by mental self-indulgence has doomed herself to incapacity for reading anything but a ceaseless round of novels, whose plots she knows beforehand, from long and dreary experience. I doubt if she could possibly be as much bored if, earlier, she had forced herself to read "the books no gentleman's library should be without."

To the fear of being bored, you may add vanity as another incentive to reading. You have no idea how often you will feel hot in ordinary conversation if you are content to preserve invincible ignorance; while, on the other hand, if you persevere in reading, you will daily feel more and more force in De Quincey's plea for books as "increasing the power of enforcing one's claims by conversation and letter."

Of course wherever you find Charybdis, Scylla is not far off, and the conversation and letter based on conscientious reading will, very likely, make the receiver sigh for " the ounce of mother-wit," which is said to be " worth a pound of clergy " (*i.e.* learning). Mother-wit is not always to be had, but, fortunately, humility is an equal safeguard against priggishness. Besides, you will be fairly safe if you never hand on, as your own, opinions which you have gleaned from reviews or magazines, and if you never give anecdotes or information. " Never tell people how you are," said a very shrewd old woman of the world; " they don't want to know." Perhaps she was unnecessarily distrustful, but all the same, there is wisdom for everyday use in a caution given to a barrister, which ran thus: "Witnesses should be kept as far away as possible from subjects in which they are especially conversant: for juries have no more relish than other people for being instructed. In every proof the witness gives of his own knowledge, they are quick to see also an unmannerly discovery of their own ignorance."

Girls are very ready to label themselves " unbookish." Some do it from a lurking idea that it will add to their charms. I freely grant that in Society charm avails a girl more than bookishness, but the absence of bookishness does not necessarily involve the presence of charm! Many more say,

"Oh, I never read; I'm not clever," with an air of sweet humility, which, translated into plain English, means, "I won't read because I can't distinguish myself,"—the smallest of all small reasons for neglecting to develop a side of the nature God gave us. Or, it means, "I won't read because it is too much trouble, and so, I will be more brainless than I need be, and less fit to do God's work."

There's the rub! You have most certainly got a vocation and a ministry awaiting you in your future life : will you be fit to undertake them when the way is opened? Dare we leave even one of our tools unsharpened when we know not what work is in store for us? "God Almighty has no need of human learning," said the popular preacher to Dr. South. "Sir," was the reply, "He has still less need of human ignorance." We dishonour God and His work by acting as if a few good resolutions and emotions were enough stock-in-trade for His workers. He needs every power we have or can acquire, and I put no limit to our possibilities of acquiring powers, if we only care enough to do it. Remember you are bound "to love the Lord your God with all your mind," and that mind is probably a much poorer thing than it need be!

No one over-values bookishness less than I do, or more regrets the selfishness which often accompanies it, but no one rates more highly than I do the value of bookishness in sharpening God's tools. Self-improvement may seem to you a selfish occupation now that your school days are over. You might be more attracted to reading if I were to touch on its possibilities of immediate usefulness— such as helping brothers in holiday tasks. But though these rewards will doubtless come to many of you in the present, I purposely do not dwell on them, because I want to give weight to something that many girls find it hard to realize,—that is, the unselfishness of using for self-improvement the breathing time that comes to most between the restraints of school life and the cares of real life. You want to do a bit of good work now, and you mourn because you are of no use in the present. *I* mourn because you will be of no use in the future, if you do not use this quiet time for forging your armour.

Steady reading seems self-ending, but when you think of all the work in the world which wants doing, and of how inadequate you are, as you now stand, for such high service, surely in every half-hour of study, in every effort to be thorough and to look things out, you are, so far as in you lies, working for what should be the object of all advancement of learning, "the glory of God and the relief of man's estate."[1]

[1] Bacon's "Advancement of Learning."

LIST OF BOOKS.

HISTORY.

Short History of the English People	GREEN	8s. 6d.
St. Louis	JOINVILLE	2s. 6d.
Chronicles	FROISSART	3s. 6d.
Siècle de Louis XIV.	VOLTAIRE	3s. 6d.
French Revolution	CARLYLE	2s. od.
Holy Roman Empire	BRYCE	7s. 6d
Germany (Story of the Nations)	BARING GOULD	5s. od.
Conquests of Granada and Spain. 2 vols.	WASHINGTON IRVING	2s. od.
Ferdinand and Isabella	PRESCOTT	5s. od.
Charles V.	,,	5s. od.
Cloister Life of Charles V.	Sir W. STIRLING MAXWELL	
Philip II.	PRESCOTT	5s. od.
Mexico	,,	5s. od.
Peru	,,	15s. od.
Dutch Republic	MOTLEY	3s. 6d.
The Makers of Florence	Mrs. OLIPHANT	10s. 6d.
,, ,, Venice	,, ,,	10s. 6d.
,, ,, Rome	,, ,,	21s. od.
Outline History of Italy	Miss SEWELL	2s. 6d.
Plutarch's Lives		s. h.
Rome (School History)	MERIVALE	3s. 6d.
Greece	OMAN	4s. 6d.
Great Rebellion	CLARENDON	s. h.
Reign of Queen Anne	STANHOPE	s. h.
,, ,, ,,	Mrs. OLIPHANT	8s. 6d.
Historical Sketches of Geo. II.	,, ,,	6s. o l.
Peninsular War	NAPIER	7s od.

TRAVELS.

Through Brittany and Normandy	K. MACQUOID *each*	7s. 6d.
Travels in France . . .	ARTHUR YOUNG	3s. 6d.
Roof of France . . .	M. B. EDWARDES	7s. 6d.
Holidays in Eastern France .	,, ,,	7s. 6d.
Holidays in Western France .	,, ,,	7s. 6d.
With a Donkey in the Cevennes	R. L. STEVENSON	2s. 6d.
Gatherings from Spain . .	FORD . . .	3s. 6d.
Bible in Spain	BORROW . .	2s. 0d.
The Land of the Magyar. 2 vols.	Mrs. N. E. MAZU-	
	CHELLI . .	s. h.
Sketches of Life in Hungary .	MARG. FLETCHER	7s. 6d.
Land beyond the Forest . .	Miss GERARD .	s. h.
Russia	WALLACE . .	5s. 0d.
Forest Life in Norway and		
Sweden	NEWLAND . .	s. h.
Residence in Norway . .	LAING . .	s. h.
Travels	MARCO POLO .	3d.
The Naturalist on the Prowl .	E. H. A. . .	7s. 6d.
Tropical Africa . . .	Prof. DRUMMOND	3s. 6d.
Where Three Empires Meet .	KNIGHT . .	3s. 6d.
England and Egypt . .	Sir A. MILNER .	7s. 6d.
Eothen	KINGLAKE . .	6s. 0d.
Land and the Book . . .	THOMSON . .	7s. 6d.
Arabia	PALGRAVE . .	6s. 0d.
Mecca	Sir R. BURTON .	6s. 0d.
Le Desért	P. LOTI . .	2s. 6d.
The Chronicles of the Sid .	ADELA ORPEN .	7s. 6d.
An Enchanted Island . .	MALLOCK . .	6s. 0d.
Curzon's Monasteries in the		
Levant		2s. 6d.
Travels in China and Thibet .	L'ABBÉ HUC .	s. h.
Malay Archipelago . . .	A. WALLACE .	6s. 0d.
Naturalist on the Amazon .	T. H. BATES .	2s. 6d.

Sandwich Islands	Miss BIRD	7s. 6d.
Voyage of a Naturalist	DARWIN	2s. 0d.
Naturalist in La Plata	HUDSON	s. h.
Recollections of a Happy Life. 2 vols.	Miss NORTH	s. h.
West Indies	FROUDE	2s. 6d.
Oceana	,,	2s. 6d.
At Last	KINGSLEY	3s. 6d
Travels	HAKLUYT	3d.
The Bow of Ulysses	PALGRAVE	s. h.

BIOGRAPHY.

Essays in Ecclesiastical Biography	Sir J. STEPHEN	7s. 6d.
S. François d'Assisi	PAUL SABATIER	14s. 0d.
S. Francis of Assisi	Mrs. OLIPHANT	6s. 0d.
S. Anselm	CHURCH	5s. 0d.
Memoirs of Col. Hutchinson	LUCY HUTCHINSON	3s. 6d.
Walton's Lives		s. h.
French Women of Letters	Miss KAVANAGH	s. h.
Angélique Arnauld	Miss MARTIN	4s. 6d.
Portraits de Femmes	SAINT BEUVE	3s. 6d.
Life of Johnson	BOSWELL	3s. 6d.
Charlotte Brontë	Mrs. GASKELL	1s. 6d.
Life of Dr. Arnold	STANLEY	2s. 0d.
Kingsley's Life		6s. 0d.
Life of Lord Lawrence	BOSWORTH SMITH	21s. 0d.
Life of Sir Henry Lawrence	Sir H.B. EDWARDES	12s. 0d.
Letters of Edward Denison	Sir B. LEIGHTON	1s. 0d.
Autobiography of Sir H. Taylor		s. h.
Life and Letters of Dean Church	M. C. CHURCH	6s. 0d.
Memorials of Charlotte Williams Wynn		s. h.
Remains of Mrs. R. Trench		6s. 0d.
Jesuits in North America	F. PARKMAN	5s. 0d.

ESSAYS.

Meditations	MARCUS AURE-		
.	LIUS .	.	1s. 6d.
Essays	BACON .	.	1s. 6d.
Gracian's Manual (Gold: Tr: Series)	.	.	2s. 6d.
Addison's Essays . ,,	. . .	net	2s. 6d.
Chesterfield's Letters ,,	. . .	.	2s. 6d.
Selections from Landor ,,	. . .	.	2s. 6d.
Essays of Elia . . .	. . .	.	1s. 6d.
Confessions of an Opium			
Eater	DE QUINCEY	.	1s. 6d.
Sketches of Moral Philosophy	SYDNEY SMITH		3s. 6d.
Essays	HAZLITT .	.	1s. 6d.
Recollections of a Literary Life	Miss MITFORD	.	6s. 0d.
Essays	MACAULAY	.	2s. 0d.
Friends in Council . . .	HELPS .	.	7s. 6d.
Guesses at Truth . . .	HARE .	.	2s. 6d.
Essays on Social Subjects .	Miss MOZLEY	.	s. h.
Heroes and Hero Worship .	CARLYLE .	.	1s. 0d.
Sartor Resartus . . .	,,	.	1s. 0d.
Past and Present . . .	,,	.	1s. 0d.
Sesame and Lilies . . .	RUSKIN .	net	5s 0d.
Twenty Essays . . .	EMERSON .	.	1s. 6d.
My Study Windows . .	LOWELL .	.	1s. 6d.
Autocrat of the Breakfast Table	HOLMES .	.	1s. 0d.
Notes on Life	Sir H. TAYLOR .		5s. 0d.
,, ,, Books . . .	,, ,,	.	5s. 0d.
Historical and Theological			
Essays	J. B. MOZLEY	.	24s. 0d
The Value of Life . . .	C. E. BURKE	.	1s. 0d.
Miscellanies, Political and Lite-			
rary	GRANT-DUFF	.	7s. 6d.
Literary and Theological Essays	W. HUTTON	,	3s. 6d.
Literary Studies . . .	W. BAGEHOT	,	3s. 6d.

Defence of Poesy . . .	Sir P. SIDNEY .	3*d*
The Compleat Angler . .	I. WALTON .	3*d.*
Religio Medici . . .	Sir T. BROWNE .	3*d.*
History of French Literature .	SAINTSBURY .	10*s.* 6*d.*
Dante	CHURCH . .	5*s.* 0*d.*
Dante, his Times and his World	A. J. BUTLER .	3*s.* 6*d.*
Readings on The Purgatorio .	W. VERNON .	24*s.* 0*d.*
Ditto, on The Inferno . .	,, .	31*s.* 6*d.*
The Shadow of Dante . .	MARIA ROSSETTI	3*s.* 6*d.*
The Study of Words . .	TRENCH . .	5*s.* 0*d.*
English Men of Letters Series .	. . . *each*	1*s.* 0*d.*
Foreign Classics Series . .	. . *each*	2*s.* 6*d.*
Ancient Classics Series . .	. . *each*	2*s.* 6*d.*
Tales of Ancient Greece . .	COXE . . .	6*s.* 0*d.*
Crito and Phædo . . .	PLATO . .	3*d.*

ART, &c.

Five Great Painters . . .	Lady EASTLAKE	*s. h.*
Old Masters	S. TYTLER . .	4*s.* 6*d.*
Modern Painters . . .	RUSKIN . .	4*s.* 6*d.*
Early Christian Art . . .	Lord LINDSAY .	*s. h.*
Greek and Gothic . . .	R. TYRWHITT .	*s. h.*
Christian Iconography . .	DIDRON . .	10*s.* 0*d.*
Frondes Agrestes . . .	RUSKIN . *net*	3*s.* 0*d.*
Stones of Venice . . .	,, ,,	10*s.* 0*d.*
Seven Lamps of Architecture .	,, ,,	7*s.* 6*d.*
A.B.C. of Architecture . .	PARKER . .	3*s.* 0*d.*
Art of Music	PARRY . .	4*s.* 6*d.*
Studies of Great Composers .	,, . .	6*s.* 0*d.*
Studies in Modern Music I. II.	W. H. HADOW .	7*s.* 6*d.*
Introductory Studies in Greek Art	J. E. HARRISON	10*s.* 6*d.*

"WHAT is one man's meat is another man's poison," and when we remember the harm we often see caused by bad novels, or even by the bad use of those which are good, we cannot wonder that many people object to them altogether. Perhaps it is owing to the prejudice often felt by good people against novels as such, that we find so many who seem to look on them as outside the domain of conscience : they would not read a bad or atheistical book of another sort, but they seem to fancy that the recording angel takes no heed, during their novel-reading time, of *what* novel they take up. They have the same half-apologetic feeling of pardonable waste of time, whether they are reading one which raises their whole standard of life, or, some rubbish which weakens and perhaps defiles their minds for months to come.

We cannot always choose our company in life ; let us resolve that, in our books at least, we will live only with the best. But if we have accustomed ourselves to "low company," "good society" cannot fail to be irksome, whether it be that of people or of books. If we find Scott and Thackeray and Miss Austen dull, and turn with relief to a circulating library, are we contentedly to accept it as an inevitable fact that we have no taste for classics? By no means! It is not enough to say, "I like this," and, "I dislike that;" we have to see to it that we like what is good and strong and wholesome, and that we dislike the reverse; if we have been lax in the matter, it is our duty to set to work and try to raise our taste. Bad taste is not a misfortune but a fault.

In this, as in all other efforts to reach a higher level, it is waste of energy to pitch our scale too high suddenly. If we enjoy sensational stories, it is absurd to limit ourselves to masterpieces; we are sure, after a more or less conscientious and weary effort, to return to yellow-backed novels with settled despair of ever enjoying better things. Common sense, and gradual progress, are as necessary in mental convalescence as in physical. If we are conscious of need for improvement in our choice of novel-reading, let us take a more practicable good resolution than abstinence; let us resolve to sandwich our books. There is a long array of novels which are admitted by all to be among the best books in our language, considered from a literary point of view, books which every cultivated person is bound to have read. Let us make a list of these, and resolve that, for every sensational novel we read, we will conscientiously get through one of those on our list before we open another of the sort we enjoy. We shall soon find that our taste is insensibly raised; that the bad tone of the inferior book will come to jar upon us when always seen in contrast with good writing.

To this personal good resolution let us add another : a resolution to keep modern fiction, as far as possible, out of the schoolroom. It is right and fitting that those who are living in the world of to-day should study its tendency and teaching in its novels, if so be that they " sandwich " them with a due proportion of the older ones that can hardly now be matched. But why begin at once to feed upon exciting stories, beside which the delicacy and reserve of Miss Austen, the history and antiquarianism of Scott, must seem cold and dry ? There is a vivid power of realization in youth, that can clothe the driest bones ; if it is not swamped by the sensational stories, which, while they seem to stimulate the imagination, in reality stunt it, by leaving it no play.

Whether we are old or young, novels may serve a most important purpose in our self-education. Do not fictitious characters read us practical lessons about our own faults, which would produce much irritation if given in words by our friends? " Westward Ho ! " preaches to us of true manliness, and

" Wives and Daughters " of true womanliness, as do few sermons. Good novels should surely greatly increase our insight into character and that power of discriminating motives, which is needed if we are not to produce " confusion worse confounded " in the many tangles of life that are sure to come in our way. Miss Edgeworth is usually considered too dull to read, but if you read her with a view to worldly wisdom, you would be surprised to find how many of her remarks would help to save you from burning your own fingers.

Dickens' humour may or may not amuse you, but if you read him with a view to the study of types, you will notice that though he probably paints no one person whom you will ever meet, yet that, more and more, you will get to classify people as " belonging to the type of so and so in Dickens."

Even more than Dickens, Miss Austen is a writer for individual taste,—one must pity and not blame those who cannot read her.   I feel inclined, however, to insist, at the sword's point, on all novel-reading being based on Scott and Mrs. Gaskell. With scarcely any exceptions, I would compel the would-be novel-reader to qualify by an examination in those two. If two additional authors were to be chosen by the candidate, I should, in my own case, offer Miss Austen and Nathaniel Hawthorne, but I could not insist on these as a matter of principle.

I was interested by seeing a series of foreign novels recommended as a form of spiritual Baedeker or Murray, for the various countries which had produced them. Guide-books are dull reading unless you have been, or are going, to their scenes, but novels which give the atmosphere of a country are as good as Prince Hussein's carpet, and almost save you the trouble of going in person. " Virgin Soil " by Tourgenieff, " Dead Souls " by Gogol, take you to Russia,— ' The Prairie," and " The Last of the Mohicans," to the backwoods,— with a vividness which is missed by some who go to the very places. Travel is supposed to enlarge the mind; with a judicious course of such novels, I would undertake to do as much for those many descendants of the Vicar of Wakefield whose " migrations are only from the blue bed to the brown ! "

If change of scene stimulates our minds, surely change of *time* does the same. I suppose the mere facts of history do us some good—but I am sure its spirit does a great deal. We find in the study of history a change of atmosphere which puts our own affairs into truer proportion, and in studying the feelings and difficulties of our predecessors, our sympathies are widened for our contemporaries. Much of this good effect of history may be arrived at through the easier medium of historical novels. Marlborough owed his English History to

Shakespeare, and ours might gain much from a series of plays and novels, perhaps beginning with " Harold " (which is said to have made Professor Freeman an historian), while Ainsworth and G. P. R. James—so unjustly laughed out of fashion by Thackeray—would fill up many gaps left by Scott and Shakespeare.   Taking such novels in order would give you a very fair knowledge of the facts which you would perhaps find dull in undiluted history, and if any one objects that they are inaccurate, I would reply that a modern " History School" would probably object quite as much to the accuracy of any history not written by its own members.

But to gain, not the facts of a past age, but its atmosphere, we must read its own novels.   A Bedouin proverb says," A man is more the child of the age in which he lives, than of his own father." We might truly say a novel is more the production of its age than of its own author.

It would be an interesting branch of the study of social history to pick out the novels which have, in turn, been representative of the young life of their day.   Clarissa Harlowe and Evelina would have headed the procession in sedan chairs: Waverley would have ridden past, heralding a whole world of feudal romance and high-mindedness.   Mr. Pickwick would then have driven up in a stage coach with Sam Weller and Mark Tapley and Mr. Pecksniff, a motley and delightful crew, to whom the very language of Waverley would have been an utterly unknown tongue.

Becky Sharpe would next have driven by, with the horses coveted by Lady Bareacres, and then the lash of the whip in " Uncle Tom's Cabin " would have diverted attention to more realistic, if not more real sorrows, than Rawdon Crawley's disillusionment and Becky's feelings when Sir Pitt proposed too late.

In 1855 the " Heir of Redclyffe" began that series of photographs of real life (only second to Miss Austen's for their value to the future historian) where you will search in vain for inaccuracies in observation of English home life or English landscape.

In ten years' time girls had deserted the chivalry and churchmanship of Guy Morville for the passionate outpourings of such books as " Comin' thro' the Rye,"—a literature which is rendered quite harmless, and even instructive, if it be read aloud to an unsympathetic elder.

Early in the " seventies " " Middlemarch " was reigning supreme, a book in which the many noble passages hid from one the fact that it depicts life as hopeless and inevitably ignoble.

Ten years later comes John Inglesant with his intangible charm, unrelated to either the definitely instructed circle in the " Heir of Redclyffe " (for whom life is interpreted by the Catechism and the " Christian Year "), or to the strenuous moral atmosphere of " Middlemarch,"—only moral, and therefore not even moral in the long-run.

The detached mystic atmosphere in " John Inglesant " is perhaps more fascinating to kindred souls than that of any other book one could name, but it is a " horn from Elfland faintly blowing ; " [1] it is not "the music to a march that sheds a joy on duty." As you rise from reading it, you feel it almost argues coarseness of moral fibre to be quite clear as to any definite duty whatsoever ! Such a book softens and spiritualizes the strong nature which is growing rigid in pursuit of clearly defined dutifulness ; but, if the nature be not safely fixed in the mould of Duty, such a book would be a dangerous dissolvent, and perhaps prevent the mould from ever giving permanent shape to the mind. Is it possibly more than a coincidence which caused the decade following the publication of " John Inglesant " to be marked by novels that are characterized by an unsettlement of faith and morals, which we should not find in the early years of the century ? As a sworn admirer of John Inglesant and Mary Collet, I cannot allow that they could ever do otherwise than " make for righteousness ; " but at least they mark a wave of indefiniteness in the air, which has since had other and far different results.

[1] " The Princess."

Or we might trace the various scenes on the stage of English life, by recounting the leading heroines; many varying lists might be made, but we may fairly claim the title for Clarissa and Evelina. Elizabeth Bennet and sweet Anne Eliot come next; then Diana Vernon "witched the world;" then came Beatrix Esmond, the heroine whom no man can help falling in love with; and then Amelia, the gentle heroine in white satin, who deserved admiration, and Becky Sharpe, the *confidante* in white linen, who got it. Thackeray is responsible for many heroines who stand out in our minds as entitled, by almost universal suffrage, to take their seats in this Parliament of women who exercised undoubted sway over the minds of men. Has he not also given us Ethel Newcome, that most fascinating younger sister of Diana Vernon?

To the Church movement of Ethel Newcome's day, of which she was so unconscious, she owes her younger cousins (akin to her in goodness and simplicity), Amy Herbert, and Ethel May. But Lady Kew's pupil would probably have felt more at ease with Lily Dale; yet no! the real Ethel Newcome would have preferred Romola, who was more like herself in outward appearance than those others. But I am forgetting one who would have been her special friend, Molly Gibson.

The inconvenient indefiniteness with which such women as Dorothea Cassaubon are fashioned would

D

have hindered the latter from making friends with Lily Dale, and those eminently sensible Ethels; but all whom I have named would have looked the other way had they met "Nancy" and her various successors. It is a curious sign of the times, that the same sort of people should now be living with Trilby and Dodo who, forty years ago, knew only such women as Ethel May and Ethel Newcome. Mrs. Norton is a reverse instance of this curious power of the Hour to mould the woman, if not the man. Had she lived to-day, she would hardly have written the "Lady of La Garaye." But if we give the *Zeitgeist* of the "forties" credit for that beautiful poem, it is all the more depressing to be obliged to consider Dodo as the outcome of to-day.

Stormy emotions and concise cynicism are tricks of the present hour, and caught by many a harmless creature, who, had she been born fifty years sooner, would have been a Mrs. Clarinda Singleheart. I suspect the Zeitgeist should bear the blame of many emotions, which the sufferers fondly imagine to be quite original, and even peculiar to themselves. The scenery for the soul's tragedies—and comedies—of our day is also painted by the Zeitgeist. It would be curious to analyse some representative modern novels, and to see how many of the colour-symphonies which nature is made to play are composed of a few nouns and adjectives, practically the invention of the last ten years. The scenes are well painted and in keeping with the play, but there is a sameness of "intensity" which is more wearying, when you once catch the trick of it, than even the sameness of commonplace.

Then too, as a sign of the times, notice the advanced age of our heroines. How absurdly young do both heroes and heroines of old novels appear to us : did we met them in real life, we should be conscious of a strong desire to send them back to the schoolroom—if not to whip them ! Heroines were then literally "to the manner born," for they began their career almost in the cradle. The sound judgment which characterized Cœlebs' Lucilla at eighteen, waits another ten years for its development in "maidens of our own day;" while we should bestow small sympathy on the " Emily " who, at fifteen, suffered from an ardent, though unrequited, attachment for Sir Charles Grandison; or on that other Emily, surnamed St. Aubert, who at a like tender age was held up by Mrs. Radcliffe as a model of constancy, because she was always in the garden with Valencourt, "listening to the tender notes of his oboe," and preserved a taste for that music through a long course of foreign travel and wicked counts. Had she lived now, she would have been ignominiously summoned indoors, to practise on a more prosaic instrument.

But instances of what seems to us premature development are to be found later than Richardson and Mrs. Radcliffe. Charlotte Brontĕ makes Shirley and Caroline such matured thoughtful women at twenty, that, methinks, could they be revived, they would find the present girls of that age somewhat crude. I have not read Miss Braddon's revised version of the Waverleys, but if she wished to make Scott's ideas harmonize with ours, she would have to add some ten years to the age of all his heroes, to make them interesting to modern heroines ; for Scott's heroes would now be at College, and the attachments of undergraduates are seldom taken *au grand sĕrieux.* Those whose memories can take them back thirty years, will bear me out in saying that girls then became old maids much sooner than they do now : they were out of court at one or two and twenty, while at twenty-five it was hardly recognized that they still had feelings ! In " Agatha's Husband," if I recollect rightly, Anne Valory sits apart at the picnic on the score of being twenty-nine. Nowadays she would have been, to all intents and purposes, as much a girl as any one else. There are many of Anne Valory's age receiving quite as much attention as chits of eighteen, who, unless very pretty, are less interesting ; though, had they lived a hundred years sooner, they would have fallen into Charybdis and been thought too *old* for the part of first heroine in any romance; nay, they would probably have been relegated to the post of *confidante.* I suppose the improvement in Women's Education has helped to keep the situation of "Heroine in Real Life" open to our girls for a longer time than would have been allowed to their great-grandmothers. Our girls of sixteen or seventeen would even now be equal to the tasks imposed on ancient heroines, which went little further than the social duties of wearing long curls and languishing at suitable seasons.

But look at all that is required of our heroines! Look, not only at girls in novels, but at actual girls in real life, who are still considered entitled to romance on their own account—though I fancy Lucilla and Cœlebs would have felt them to be entitled not to Romance, but to Reverence. Look, I say, at such girls now,—they have to take intelligent interest in a thousand things that Lucilla and Harriet Byron never heard of, and some of which would have scandalized those good women.

Unless a woman has the peculiar gifts which enable her to play the *rôle* of a Child of Nature, she will find it useful to possess an amount of education in Social Science, politics, etc., which cannot possibly be acquired by sixteen; consequently the limits of the Heroic Age have to be widened.

Then, too, the same result is furthered by many

present-day poets, who burn incense at the shrines
of haggard images of our Lady of Passion.   Girls
of sixteen cannot well look haggard or point to interesting lines on their brows, traced by the wan
finger of experience.   They were quite up to the
requirements of the last age, which only demanded
that its heroines should be clean and sweet and
fair, and, above all things, fresh in mind and heart
and dress.   Freshness has ceased to be the fashion
now, and, except when taken as a restorative after
the turbid seas of Passion (with a particularly large
P) which meet us in every novel, it is apt to pall
on the modern imagination,—the " Papa, Potatoes,
Prunes and Prism " of yore have given place to
Passion, Psychology, Pain and Protoplasm.   I know
not who so upset the ancient order of things, as
to bring about this change : it must have been a
woman, for no man could have been capable of
such a delicate stroke of genius !   Only a favoured
few had the natural graces formerly necessary for
aspirants to heroine-ism : but any one can look
haggard and *passée* and not much washed, which
is all that our more lenient age demands for its
heroines.   All honour to her who invented this
simple type, which saves so many deserving
heroines from superannuation !

There are many delights in store for those who
will turn to the atmosphere of a century ago,
breathed in the " Romance of the Forest " and " Sir

Charles Grandison." In these days of magazines and reviews, when every one feels bound to read the last new book, it is almost a mockery to urge the study of Mrs. Radcliffe's works, " The Italian," " The Mysteries of Udolpho " (in four thick volumes). Nevertheless, I could wish no one pleasanter company during a spell of rainy weather in the country. To be properly enjoyed, they should be read aloud; only so can you appreciate the sublime calm with which hero and heroine discourse on some such theme as the superiority of virtue to vice, while you and your hearers are quivering in expectation of a shot, remembering that the Capuchin or the Bandit (or both) crept, only two pages before, under the shadow of the neighbouring rock. The hero and the heroine always see him quite plainly, but they converse uninterruptedly, knowing, from long experience in romances, that he never fires when he has a decent chance of hitting his mark.

The race of heroines has strangely developed since Mrs. Radcliffe's days. How terribly " of the earth, earthy " do Mr. Trollope's appear, in comparison! Fresh from the society of Emily St. Aubert, it is a shock to find Lily Dale requiring her dinner at any and every crisis of her fate. Mdlle. St. Aubert, after a hard day's work of eluding wicked marquises and exploring haunted rooms, rejects a good supper with the remark : " *I* must learn to feed on sorrow." It is quite a relapse into low life when Adela orders "a light refreshment at the inn;" but, as she had spent the morning in binding up the wounds of one lover, three ruffians, and a persecutor, she had some excuse.

After living "Auf der Höhe" with Emily and Adela, it feels strange to turn again to the "light of common day" in "Sir Charles Grandison." The conversation, except for its oaths and old-world courtesy, seems an echo of our own. The expressions often raise a smile, as when the rejected lover "stept into his chariot, rearing his head up to the top of it, as he sat swelling." But we find the questions of our own day debated. Take, for example, the discussion in which Sir Charles graciously assures us that, "in Heaven, women will certainly be on a footing with men as to intellectuals," a discussion which Miss Byron closes with the sound reflection, "Surely, my Lucy, we may pronounce that where no duty is neglected, where modesty, delicacy, and a teachable spirit are preserved as characteristics of the sex, it need not be thought a disgrace for a woman to be supposed to know something."

It must be owned that Lady G. is the only person in the book free from suspicion of moving on polite wires, but then, how many *living* characters do we meet with in the novels of the present day?

And what a dreary waste do most of these novels seem to the chastened imagination that has learnt to delight in the " volant quill " of Miss Byron, which kept her ' venerable circle' in Northamptonshire so fully informed of all her London experiences. Each sigh of every lover, each thought of the heroine, are faithfully detailed to " my Lucy," for the benefit of " our Aunt Selby " and " our Grandmother Shirley," that " reverend parent " and " condescending excellence," who, after a few hours of " her Byron's society," announced her intention of returning home, remarking " that it was now fitting she should mortify after such a regale." *We* should have no time to read such letters, much less write them,—and one has to keep in mind the stationary, restful life of the days when this circle of " polite letter-writers " detailed to each other every incident and conversation.

But not only does their minuteness exceed ours in *quantity*, it takes a wholly different *form*. Miss Byron's placid autobiography has no shadow of relationship to that minuteness of George Eliot's psychological investigations, which leaves such a painful impression of dissected souls. Harriet Byron was spared any approach to George Eliot's sense of that " keen vision and feeling of all ordinary human life, which if we had it, would be like hearing the grass grow and the squirrel's heart beat, and we should die of that roar which lies on the

other side of silence." Far from being in any
danger of suffering from the "roar," Harriet Byron
was so incessantly busy in hearing or retailing
small talk and compliments, that she never can
have arrived at Silence. She has none of Dorothea's
yearnings after unattainable goodness, but rather a
comfortable sense of the duty of "doing well unto
one's self."

In these days, when the great problems of
existence are common topics of conversation, and
magazines are discussing whether "life is worth
living," it is curious to see the utter absence of
such "obstinate questionings," and "blank mis-
givings" in the society Richardson draws for us.
The Religious Instinct, the Craving after the
Infinite, take, with Sir Charles, the form of a
"cheerful piety" which impels him in church (and
throughout life) to "pay his compliments only
secondarily to his wife, feeling that his first are due
to his Maker."

The book impresses one strongly with the idea
that reticence is a modern invention. Cautions
against "opening wide the bridal chambers of the
heart"[1] would have been incomprehensible to
Harriet. In the index, under the heading, "Miss
Byron," we frequently find the entry, "describes
several tender passages between herself and Sir
Charles." In truth the most confidential speeches

[1] "Gardener's Daughter."

are made in such irreproachably " full dress " that it would be a pity to keep them from the company.

But although Harriet did not happen to have that modern possession, " a buried life," and was perfectly competent to put down in the best hand-writing " all those nameless feelings that coursed through her breast," [1] yet, to do her justice, her sentiments were irreproachable on all occasions ; she was sensible and well-informed, an intelligent companion to her husband, a good housewife, had her feelings under control, and fulfilled all the social and religious duties recognized by her age. It is true that to our age, higher and broader ideas of duty have been given, and more will therefore be required of us. Still, she will be a good and faithful servant who, in the present day, fills her larger sphere of work as conscientiously as a smaller sphere was filled by that type of old-world womanhood—Miss Harriet Byron.

But I am lingering too long over the old-fashioned novels which I delight in. I wish I could persuade you to exchange some of Mudie's new lamps for these old ones ! For I want to ask your patience while I dwell on some of the points in modern novels, which I think call for our serious attention.

One school of those novels, which I should strongly urge all girls to avoid, is that which

[1] M. Arnold.

tampers with religious faith. Some of them claim to show you a more excellent way, some of them proclaim that there is no way to be found. It is with these last that I have least patience. There is a tradition in Yorkshire that the ghosts of those who die by falling into "pot holes" haunt the moors and lure stray travellers to the same fate. The spectre with broken bones, limping beside the wayfarer and terrifying him, till he too stumbles into those awful depths, always seemed to me a most eerie conception, but it is nothing compared to the cruelty of those who disturb another's faith, having nothing to offer in exchange. It may be a relief to the writer to cry aloud that there is no answer to the riddle of life, and that, as in Heine's poem, "a fool waits for the answer," but if that is all the contribution he can make to the general need, in novel-writing or in conversation, he would be braver, as well as wiser, if he held his peace, and consumed his own smoke.

But there are some who feel they *can* offer new lamps for old ones, and who do so in "novels with a purpose." It is a curious sign of the times that these attacks on our faith are now met with in novels and magazines, which lie about on every table ; whereas in old times they would have been confined to learned treatises and addressed to a properly trained audience.

It is the lack of proper mental training in the

readers that makes these present attacks so dangerous. In one of those novels, a young man is severely commented on for declining to read unsound books. This intolerance is contrasted with the open-mindedness of the hero, who chooses his Master's adversary for a close friend, and unbelieving books for his main study. In ordinary life one does not admire a man who picks out his father's slanderer as his bosom friend—is it any more beautiful in us if we single out for friendship those who despise Christ? We know that all feeling is contagious,—have we any right to go wilfully into temptation? Giants of intellect have found that Christian evidence and theology afford scope for a life's work: is it "truth seeking" or "temptation seeking," when an untrained, unequipped mind goes into these questions? The present day is very full of distrust of old-fashioned truths, but is there enough self-distrust on the part of the truth seekers?

You say, "We should learn to give a reason for the faith that is in us." Certainly; but we had better do it under circumstances that give a fair chance to the Faith; we are so bent on being fair to the enemy, that we forget that fairness cuts both ways. It is quite as possible (and almost more frequent nowadays) to be narrow-minded and illiberal on the anti-Christian, as on the Christian side. I quite admit that in this matter the religious world *used* to be the greatest hindrance to religion, and our cause suffers for this now, in that it is tacitly assumed there will be more generosity and justice in the opponent than in the defender of Christianity. I protest against the unfairness of stories which endow atheists with all the Christian graces, and the orthodox with that intolerance which, in real life, is not confined to either side.

But it is not only their unfairness that would make me put such novels on an index,—it is the discussion of difficulties before a mixed audience, that I feel to be so dangerous. Not because the truth will not bear handling, but because we are not fit to handle it. We shall all agree with Milton, when he says, "'Though all the winds of doctrine were let loose to play upon the earth, so Truth be in the field we do ingloriously . . . to misdoubt her strength." But I do not go on to echo his consequent plea for liberty of printing, since I should like to have these questions argued in Latin. It is not truth, but her followers, who sometimes cannot stand these winds.

A young man is not supposed to be in a position to judge for himself in science till after a long scientific training. Very little sympathy would be bestowed on him if he broke his heart at the outset of his career, because he was quite sure Huxley and Tyndall were on a wrong track, as " one of his lectures had said so," and " he had seen it in print " ! But I have known people declare against religion on no better evidence—mainly, indeed, from a wish to stand on their own feet !—it is the extreme weakness of those feet that makes me object to the attitude. Far from these doubts being more intellectual than the simple faith in which one was brought up, it seems to me most crudely unintellectual to imagine one's self qualified to pronounce an original opinion, without theological and evidential training, which only the most exceptional women possess. If you are prepared to undergo the training, well and good; if not, it seems to me a duty not to choose books which attack the Faith, in whose defence we have been too indolent to arm ourselves.

Some read these books on the plea that going through the dark places will help them to guide others. If God sends you an illness, you can afterwards by your knowledge help others who go through the same, but you would not willingly run into infection merely to enlarge your experience. Common sense would tell you not to face such a certain risk for the sake of a very doubtful good to others. Why are we to think more lightly of risk to our souls? If there were any certain good for others gained by this search after experience I would say nothing; but *is* there? Does any one but God know " what is in the darkness"? Are not the " dark places " peculiar to each one? Can any

human soul touch any other soul in these things?
"Language conceals thought," and the would-be
guide is pretty sure to miss the real perplexity.
Only the Great Physician can give the real remedy
—another would but catch the disease and not help
the patient.

There are some who must pass through the
Valley of the Shadow of Doubt, but I am speaking
of those who from intellectual curiosity, or a wish
to be in the intellectual fashion of the day, deliberately go into that valley. Is it not more helpful to
keep a clean bill of health yourself and to stand
outside the Dark Valley, shining in the sunlight,
and showing, as Faithful did to Christian, that outside the valley there are "workers, lovers all about,"[1]
and that the Valley is only a small part of life?
Surely feeling is contagious, and argument is not,—
your argument cannot have quite the same shade
of meaning for your hearer as for you—ten to one
you miss the point for *him*. But, to know that
another is facing life dutifully and bravely, in a
strength that the Doubter cannot yet realize, gives
him a feeling that strength *does* exist somewhere—
that the sun is shining on some part of God's
empire, though perhaps not at that moment on his
own garden.

These novels which may unsettle our faith will
be avoided by those who realise what their effect

[1] "Within and Without" (G. MacDonald).

may be. But there is a still larger class of seemingly harmless trash, which is often looked upon as a neutral ground where conscience has nothing to say. I am not sure of this being a true view. Surely the ground of our Lord's judgment on idle words lies, not in the individual word itself, but in its being the index to an idle mind. May we conscientiously indulge in any habit which tends to make our minds thus idle? For a busy worker to relax occasionally over rubbish is one thing; for an idler to read nothing else, is quite another. A woman who takes to drinking is considered a sad, a scandalous, and well-nigh a hopeless case. I know some who are nearly as useless, nearly as impervious to higher influences, as if their minds' fibre had been unstrung by drink; and yet with these, it is not drink, but reading weak novels, which has done the mischief. Certainly the rest of their life matched their reading, so you may say the novels should not bear all the blame, but I think if they had kept a higher standard in reading, there would have been some grit in them to turn on to better things, when the follies of their youth left them stranded in middle age.

If we get up from a novel, dissatisfied with that state of life to which we have been called, and inclined to pity ourselves, then we may be sure that such a novel is our poison, and should be laid aside. The main use of novel-reading should be to

E

let fresh air into our lives, instead of such malaria;
novels should give us a change of air and scenery,
to send us back to our own lives with fresh vigour,
with nobler aims and hopes than before.

There are few things with regard to which it
more behoves us for our soul's health to remember
that " a light of duty shines on every day for all," [1]
than with regard to novel-reading, and there is
scarcely anything which is so seldom made a point
of conscience. If we once let our eyes dwell on
anything bad, we cannot forget it at will; it haunts
us for years, and comes back when we most long
to be free from it—and yet many would read of
evil which they would shrink from hearing of.
Bad novels find entrance where bad companions
would not, and yet they are the more dangerous of
the two; for we more insensibly fall into the tone
of the books we read than of the people we meet,
since there is nothing, while we are reading, to
arouse our attention, or that of others, to the
gradual change in our standard which is taking
place. It is not only downright bad novels which
our conscience ought to forbid, not only those
which manifestly seek to attract by picturing evil,
and which ask our sympathy for sin, and obscure
our sense of right and wrong: there are many
which do not deserve such harsh censure, but yet
which strike us as rather profane, or rather vulgar, or

[1] "The Excursion."

rather coarse when we begin them, though there is nothing positively wrong in them. But, if we are to strive after perfection, then it is our clear duty to close such books at once; for nothing is so quickly lost as this vague sense of distaste for evil, and we may accept it as an inevitable judgment that, by the time we have read such a book through, we shall for ever have lost that full power of seeing and shrinking from its evil, which was ours when we opened it.

And yet some old-fashioned books are coarse, without quite deserving our avoidance.

My theory is that dirt does not stick after it is dry, and that old-fashioned coarseness is nothing like so hurtful as a verbally less offensive book of the present day. There are French novels which could be read out aloud quite well, and yet which would leave one with no moral sense at all.

I wish you would read *no* French novels without a warrant from some old-fashioned person—the name of the author is no guarantee at all, for the same man will write a black novel and a white one, without seeming to know the difference. Their workmanship makes most English novels seem, by comparison, perfectly childish; but I deliberately would rather a girl did not know how to read than that she should read the French novels I speak of. If she says that they do her no harm, she is like Rappacini's daughter,[1] and has learnt to breathe

[1] "Mosses from an Old Manse."

poison. They have a curious power of deadening
the moral sense, and I would almost rather she
read something that would shock her more.

Girls read many books which they say are
" powerful," an adjective which generally means
"disgusting." I do not object to strong situations
if some spiritual beauty is brought out; but I deny
that even artistic perfection is reached unless this
is done. Mere animal beauty is an anachronism—
a lackingness (if I may coin a word)—in a woman,
or in a book, that is born in this age, which has
advanced to a spiritual level unknown to the Greeks.
Browning's " Old Pictures in Florence" has a bearing on novels as well as on pictures; and I do not
think we are justified in reading a book which only
shows power of depicting animal emotions.

I think, unless a girl can say that the world and
the flesh have *no* hold over her whatsoever, she has
no right to tamper with them, by reading books
which are " earthly, sensual," though there may be
no absolute wickedness about them, which would
earn for them St. James' third adjective.

Surely, too, the moral vulgarity of many books of
the kind should be a safeguard. The housemaids'
story, whose interest lies in such " promising nouns "
as Earls and Countesses, Velvets and Diamonds, is
allowed to be vulgar. Surely (putting right and
wrong aside) there is as much moral vulgarity in
books which rely for attraction on more lurid nouns

You have no idea how often it would help another girl, who, in her heart dislikes that kind of thing, if you had the courage to show that you *do* mind what you read, and that you are content to take an elder's advice, instead of investigating for yourself. God shelters many from evil, and it is one of the chief "blessings of this life" when He does; but some seem to think it selfish and ignoble to remain sheltered, when others are not. Possibly it is ignoble to eat my dinner to-day, when some one else goes hungry. If I could transfer my dinner to him, it would perhaps be nobler. But to burn my dinner, in order to put myself on his level, would bear no "signs of nobleness" about it; it would only weaken my power of serving him after dinner.

Girls tarnish their own purity by reading and talking of evil, with a vague idea of helping in some grand struggle for good. Reading doubtful novels, and acquiring the debased form of that very useful possession "knowledge of the world," is not the way to win the power of one with whom "men at her side grow nobler—girls purer." The longer I live the more convinced I am that nothing you say, or do, has any effect compared to the "virtue" which goes out of you unconsciously, for good or for ill, according to what you *are*. Every doubtful book that you read kills a certain amount of the virtue of purity, which might have come out of you,

and might have helped some one in their battle
against evil, of which you may be unconscious.
By every such book you deliberately put a veil
between your soul and the Beatific Vision. You
cannot be as much shocked at the end of a book
which offends your taste, or your sense of right and
wrong, as you were at the beginning : such indul-
gence must blunt our feelings.

Some speak contemptuously of "cloistered
virtue." I never find that people afflicted with
temper seek annoyances, or that the proud seek
mortifications, for fear their virtue should be
"cloistered." In such matters they trust God to
supply them with sufficient exercise in their " daily
round." But in the matter of purity, they "rush
in" where greater saints have "feared to tread."
Is it because they want an excuse for eating the
fruit that Eve also thought "was to be desired"?
They sometimes call it selfish and cowardly to "go
through life with their eyes shut." It seems to
me that the "open eyes," which they think so
meritorious, mean wilful staring at various ugly
things which lie outside their natural line of vision.

"A tree to be desired to make one wise."
These words go home to us as much as to Eve;
more so, I think, as the world is more complex
now, and knowledge of the world is consequently
more interesting.

SUGGESTIONS FOR NOVEL READING.

(EXCLUDING HISTORICAL STORIES.)

BOOKS "IT BECOMES A YOUNG WOMAN TO KNOW."

The Waverley Novels . . .	Sir W. Scott.
Sir C. Grandison	Richardson.
Marriage	Miss Ferrier.
Destiny	,, ,,
Inheritance	,, ,,
Miss Austen's Novels.	
Ennui	Miss Edgeworth.
Patronage	,, ,,
Helen	,, ,,
Villette	C. Brontë.
Shirley	,,
Deerbrook	Miss Martineau.
Cranford	Mrs. Gaskell.
Wives and Daughters . . .	,, ,,
Sylvia's Lovers	,, ,,
North and South	,, ,,
The Spy	F. Cooper.
Last of the Mohicans . . .	,,
The Prairie	,,
The Pathfinder	,,
Esmond	Thackeray.
Newcomes	,,
Martin Chuzzlewit	Dickens.
Bleak House	,,
Our Mutual Friend . . .	,,
The Caxtons	Bulwer Lytton.
My Novel	,, ,,
Never too Late to Mend . .	C. Reade.

Scenes of Clerical Life	. .	G. ELIOT.
Romola		,,
Silas Marner		,,
Westward Ho !		C. KINGSLEY.
Hypatia		,,
Ravenshoe.		H. KINGSLEY.
Transformation		N. HAWTHORNE.
House with the Seven Gables	.	,,
The Experience of Life .	.	Miss SEWELL.
Barchester Towers . .	.	A. TROLLOPE.
Last Chronicles of Barset .	.	,,
The Daisy Chain . .	.	Miss YONGE.
Heart's-ease		,, ,,
Clever Woman of the Family	.	,, ,,
Robert Falconer. . .	.	G. MACDONALD.
Miss Majoribanks . .	.	Mrs. OLIPHANT.
The Beleaguered City .	.	,, ,,
Noblesse Oblige. . .	.	S. FRASER-TYTLER.
Lorna Doone . . .	.	R. BLACKMORE.
John Inglesant . . .	.	H. SHORTHOUSE.

"SANDWICH" BOOKS.[1]

Too Strange not to be True	.	Lady G. FULLERTON.
Kenelm Chillingly . .	.	BULWER LYTTON.
Coningsby. . . .	.	DISRAELI.
Sybil		,,
Tancred		,,
Lothaire		,,
Ivan de Biron . . .	.	Sir A. HELPS.
Casimir Maremma . .	.	,, ,,
Realmah		,, ,,
Heir of Redclyffe . .	.	Miss YONGE.

[1] See p. 26.

Dynevor Terrace . . .	Miss YONGE.
Can you forgive her ? . .	A. TROLLOPE.
The Small House at Allington.	,,
Phineas Finn	,,
Old Town Folk . . .	Mrs. BEECHER STOWE.
The Minister's Wooing . .	,, ,,
Katie Brand	HOLME LEE.
Nathalie	Miss KAVANAGH.
Adéle	,, ,,
Ferneyhurst Court . . .	Lady VERNEY.
Castle Daly	Miss KEARY.
Janet's Home	,, ,,
Gayworthys	A. D. J. WHITNEY.
A Maiden of our own Day .	F. W. WILFORD.
Sir Gibbie	G. MacDONALD.
For the Right	FRANZOS.
Madonna of a Day . . .	Miss DOUGALL.
Days of Yore	S. FRASER TYTLER.

FOR "THE LAND WHERE IT IS ALWAYS AFTERNOON."

Semi-detached House . .	Hon. E. EDEN.
Semi-attached Couple . .	,, ,,
Charles O'Malley . . .	C. LEVER.
Harry Lorrequer . . .	,,
Cruise upon Wheels . .	C. A. COLLINS.
The Moonstone . . .	W. COLLINS.
The Coming Race . . .	BULWER LYTTON.
Christowell	R. BLACKMORE.
Alice Lorraine . . .	,,
Off the Skelligs . . .	JEAN INGLELOW.
For Percival	MARGARET VELEY.
Mitchelhurst Place . . .	,, ,,

But yet a Woman . .	A. S. HARDY.
Denise	Miss ROBERTS.
May	Mrs. OLIPHANT.
Lady Car	„ „
Véra	C. L. H. DEMPSTER.
Hôtel du Petit S. Jean .	„ „
Dorothy Fox . . .	Mrs. PARR.
Prophet of the Great Smoky Mountain. . . .	M. N. MURFREE.
Ramona	H. JACKSON.
Reata	Miss GERARD.
Orthodox	„
Recha	„
A Family Affair . . .	H. CONWAY.
Mr. Smith	Mrs. WALFORD.
The Refugees . . .	CONAN DOYLE.
A Daughter of Heth . .	BLACK.
Adventures of a Phæton .	„
Princess of Thule . .	„
Village on the Cliff . .	Miss THACKERAY.
Old Kensington . . .	„ „
Initials	Baroness TAUTPHŒUS.
Quits	„ „
Day Book of Mrs. Bethia Hardacre. . . .	Mrs. FULLER MAITLAND.
Saltonstall Gazette . .	„ „

IN " Romola " we learn to know, not only
Florence, but the fifteenth century with " its
strange web of belief and unbelief, with its zeal for
old manuscripts, and its waxen images hanging up
under the protection of the Madonna Annunziata ; "
—we see " the incomparable Lorenzo, with the dim
outward eyes and the subtile inward vision ; " and
the Prior of San Marco, Savonarola, who " had the
greatness which belongs to a life spent in struggling
against powerful wrong, and in trying to raise men
to the highest deeds they are capable of." And,
though we are thus brought face to face with the
actors in one of the greatest dramas of history, yet
the book teaches us " the broad sameness of the
human lot, which never alters in the main headings
of its history—hunger and labour, seedtime and
harvest, love and death."

" Romola " is a careful study of place and time,
and may well teach more, both of history and
geography, than many a text-book or careless
travel, but yet the predominant impression it leaves
on one's mind is that of much-needed lessons for

our own lives :—the nobleness of Truth and Duty, of that " great gift of the gods, to be born with a hatred and contempt of all injustice and meanness ; " the truth of " that inexorable law of human souls, that we prepare ourselves for sudden deeds, by the reiterated choice of good or evil, that really determines character."

The possibilities of beauty in life have been heightened for all of us who know the blind old scholar Bardo, and his daughter Romola,—" such a woman as the immortal poets had a vision of when they sang the lives of the heroes—tender but strong, like her voice which was to him instead of the light in the years of his blindness." Into their studious life entered the beautiful young Greek, Tito Melema, supple in mind and body—and soul. His bright face, with its rich tinted beauty, was " like a wreath of spring, dropped suddenly in Romola's young but wintry life, which had inherited nothing but memories—memories of a dead mother, of a lost brother, of a blind father's happier time,— memories of far-off light, love and beauty, that lay imbedded in dark mines of books."

Bardo sought Tito's aid in the learned work which was to be the blind man's title to fame. " He looked so bright and gentle : he must feel as she did, that, in this eagerness of blind age, there was piteousness enough to call for the inexhaustible patience. . . . . A girl of eighteen imagines the feelings behind the face that has moved her with its sympathetic youth, as easily as primitive people imagined the humours of the gods in fine weather." In Romola's presence, Tito's responsive nature was in tune with hers, for "each woman creates in her own likeness the love tokens that are offered her." But his past life is sullied by base denial of the foster-father who rescued him from slavery, and his present is entangled by deceiving the peasant girl Tessa—half from kindliness, half from the drifting towards the softest corner, which is the fatal flaw in his nature.

Surely in no other book do we find such a marvellous study of character, or rather of temperament, as this of Tito. Every one in whose nature lies the smallest tinge of pleasure-seeking should read the story of the unintended misery which his shrinking from disagreeables brought on himself and all around him.

Every woman to whom "the cross comes as a wife, should learn to carry it as a wife," from the lessons taught to Romola by Savonarola. Should I not rather say, that every woman should lay to heart his words, "The higher life begins for us, my daughter, when we renounce our own will to bow before a Divine law. That seems hard to you. It is the portal of wisdom, and freedom, and blessedness. That wisdom is the religion of the cross"? Romola learnt her lesson

and made her life fair with " beautiful loving deeds,
rescuing those who were ready to perish," " though
there is no compensation for the woman who feels
that the chief relation of her life has been no more
than a mistake. She has lost her crown. The
deepest secret of human blessedness has half
whispered itself to her, and then for ever passed
her by."

At first sight, Romola's simple majesty and
high-minded goodness win our whole sympathy, as
contrasted with the baseness of the man whom she
credited with a like nobility of soul. But we miss
much of the tragedy of the story, if we overlook
the fact that she and Tito represent the opposite
temperaments of north and south. It is not merely
the contrast of virtue and vice; it is a study of the
disastrous effect of the contact of two natures,
which each brought out the fault of the other.
Tito developed the hardness which is too often the
deadly sin of women of Romola's type; while her
very virtues crushed his sympathetic responsive
nature as with a cloak of lead.

The story of her love and its betrayal is inter-
woven with that of the great Dominican monk,
who ruled Florence in virtue of " his burning
indignation at the sight of wrong; of his fervent
belief in an unseen Justice that would put an end
to the wrong, and in an unseen Purity to which
lying and uncleanness were an abomination." In

the midst of his powerful denunciations of the sins
of Florence and the corruptions of the Church, he
found time to save Romola from despair. " No
soul is desolate so long as there is a human being
for whom it can feel trust and reverence. . . . The
first condition of human goodness is something
to love ; the second, something to reverence."
Savonarola supplied Romola with both these conditions, for his mind never stopped short of the
sublimest end. . . . Even in the last terrible days,
when ignominy, torture, and the fear of torture had
laid bare every hidden weakness of his soul, he
would say to his importunate judges : " do not
wonder if it seems to you that I have told you but
few things ; for my purposes were few and great."

I have touched on the main characters and main
themes of the story, as much as possible in the
words of the book, because no description would
give so forcible an idea, as does exact quotation,
of the noble words and poetic rhythm in which
that story is told. The reader lives, for the time
being, in a city which is the joy of the whole earth
for its beauty and for its memories; he moves
among famous men of old, but the great charm of
the book is that it interprets for us some of the
painful riddles of our own life, that it leaves " our
heart beating faster at the sight of generous deeds."
We feel no doubt as we read, " what is the highest
prize the soul can win ; we almost believe in our

own power to attain it;" we rise in spirit to the
heights on which Romola stood when she said, "It
is a poor sort of happiness that could ever come by
caring very much about our own narrow pleasures.
We can only have the highest happiness, by having
wide thoughts and much feeling for the rest of the
world as well as ourselves: and this sort of
happiness often brings so much pain with it, that
we can only tell it from pain by its being what
we would choose before everything else."

Charles Kingsley.

PERHAPS few things would have given so much pleasure to this "true lover," Charles Kingsley, as to have known that his wife would have a larger share than he himself in making his name famous. Mrs. Kingsley's life of her husband made him a household name to even a wider circle than had been charmed by his books. I know of no other wife, except perhaps Lucy Hutchinson, to whom it has been given to force the world to look at her husband through her eyes.

"Romeo and Juliet" is perhaps the most famous version of the first act of that often-played drama of "the world's great bridals," but the married life of Charles Kingsley, as pictured in this book, is worthy to be taken as an unsurpassed second act, while I cannot think of any third and final act, except "By the Fire-side."

No wonder, when he had such a home as Eversley, that "faith in womankind" was Kingsley's watchword, and that "trust in all things high," came easy to him.

F

" If any two creatures grew into one,
    They would do more than the world has done,
    Though each apart were never so weak."

It is, therefore, no wonder that Kingsley's short fifty years of work accomplished so much, when his wife could write of him as she does :—

" If in the highest, closest of earthly relationships, a love that never failed for six and thirty years—pure, patient, passionate—a love which never stooped from its own lofty level to a hasty word, an impatient gesture, or a selfish act, in sickness or in health, in sunshine or in storm, by day or by night, could prove that the age of chivalry has not passed away for ever, then Charles Kingsley fulfilled the ideal of a 'most true and perfect knight,' to the one woman blest with that love in time and to eternity."

Few things are more touching than the closing scenes of his life, when he snatched from Death itself one last hour with her whom he had so loved and served. Surely the " love never found an earthly close " which died (or seemed to die) to such strains as theirs did—to the sound of Wordsworth's " Ode on Immortality," Matthew Arnold's " Buried Life," and Milton's " Ode to Time."

His epitaph consisted of the three words in which the life of his life, past, present, and future, is gathered up—" *Amavimus, amamus, amabimus.*"

Not Sir Lancelot or Sir Richard Grenvile was more faithful to his Lady, more gentle to the weak, more stout-hearted against all evil and oppression.

"He was ever a fighter," a man of "fierce wars and faithful loves." His last words were the sigh of relief, "No more fighting."

Well might his wife dedicate her book to the

"Beloved Memory of

A RIGHTEOUS MAN

Who loved God and Truth above all things.
A man of untarnished honour—
Loyal and chivalrous—gentle and strong—
Modest and humble—tender and true—
Pitiful to the weak—yearning after the erring—
Stern to all forms of wrong and oppression,
Yet most stern towards himself—
Who being angry, yet sinned not—
Whose highest virtues were known only
To his wife, his children, his servants and the poor.
Who lived in the presence of God here,
And passing through the Grave and Gate of death
Now liveth unto God for evermore."

The two events which coloured his whole life were his finding a home at Clovelly when he was eleven, and his marriage with Miss Grenfell when he was twenty-five.

He was a many-sided man. The muscularity of

his training, his love of dogs and horses, was no
bar to earnest loving work as a "country parson,"
who need not have shrunk from a comparison
even with George Herbert's model; while his
poetic nature gave forth, in constant flow, books
which have helped to keep Englishmen as manly
and as pure as the heroes of whom he sang in his
prose Epic, "Westward Ho!"

"The Saints' Tragedy," written when he was
twenty-nine, roused Bunsen to such a pitch of
enthusiasm, that he begged Kingsley to continue
Shakespeare's Historical Plays! But 1848 filled his
mind with the making of history, not the writing
of it. He felt "the day of the Lord at hand."

> " Every morning brought a noble chance,
>   And every chance brought forth a noble knight,"[1]

—such knights as Tom Hughes, F. D. Maurice,
Sidney Godolphin Osborne, Mansfield, Ludlow :—
Christian Socialists, shoulder to shoulder with
whom Kingsley found his work.

His papers, signed "Parson Lot," in "Politics
for the People" (among them one on Bellini's
picture of "the Doge"), "Yeast," and "Alton
Locke" show him to us, as that "Priest of God and
tribune of the People," which Dr. Arnold declared
every clergyman should be.

In 1853 came "Hypatia," with that fine gentleman,

---

[1] Tennyson.

Raphael; and then, while Crimean fighting was going on, Kingsley, to use his own expression, " wrote books to make others fight," and produced " Westward Ho !" which stands alone in its wonderful mastery of the fascination of the sea, and of Devon, and of England's forgotten worthies.

Then came the " Heroes "—Greek fairy tales, as delicate and graceful as the laughter of the many-twinkling sea. In 1857, " Two Years Ago," where he portrayed Clovelly most charmingly. Then came the " Water Babies," a very fascinating example of the modern story-book, spoken to the child, but really addressed to the nurse.

In 1860, came his work as Professor of History at Cambridge, and in 1869 as Canon of Chester, where he wrote " Madam How and Lady Why" and " At Last."

In 1873 came the canonry at Westminster and his final visit to America, from which he returned with the beginnings of the illness under which he sank in 1875, aged fifty-five.

His poems were written at various times. Professor Knight counts him as one of the greatest of our minor poets. Surely he is, for one thing, the chief of modern ballad singers; look at his spirited " North Easter," which " stirs our Vikings' blood," and the rhythm of " Loraine, Loraine, Loree." But note, too, the delicate music of " Earl Haldan's Daughter," and the pathos of the " Mango

Tree," told by the crazy desolate woman, who
loses husband and children amid the luxuriant
beauty of a tropical forest, and whose thoughts
brood over the English home, where that husband
" told his boy's love, soft and oft." Around her
are "the monkeys in their foolish strife; the
lizards basking on the soil,"—

> "But still within her foolish brain
>   There hangs a pale blue evening sky;
>   A furzy croft; a sandy lane."

One is grateful to Kingsley for speaking in the
vulgar tongue, although, when a man so evidently
means what he says and says what he means, it is
apt to slay suggestiveness and poetic half-lights.
Yet the singer of the " Night Bird" was a true
poet.

Christian Socialism had not become fashionable
in 1848, and Kingsley and his " Master" (as he
loved to called Maurice) followed her before she
walked in silver slippers.

Parson Lot, with his simple hard hitting (at the
mercy of a practised fencer like Cardinal Newman),
was a good soldier in that same army to which
Heine, in all other ways so unlike him, claimed
admission. Heine's creed might well have been
spoken by Kingsley—

> " Now that I have grown to manhood,
>   Read and travelled more than most,

Swells my heart, and I acknowledge
With full heart the Holy Ghost.

" He has wrought the mightiest marvels,
Mightier works for suffering folk ;
He cast down the barons' strongholds,
Broke for aye the villeins' yoke.

" Thousand knights in shining armour,
Of the Holy Ghost inspired,
Chosen His will to do in all things,
With great courage hath He fired.

" Now, my child, come look upon me,
Kiss me, boldly look, and boast
Thou hast looked on such a champion,
Knight, child ! of the Holy Ghost." [1]

But Nature, as well as Human Nature, owns Charles Kingsley's allegiance. De Quincey says local attachment to lovely country is a necessary constituent of happiness, and boyhood at Clovelly gave this to Kingsley. Few have so repaid their debts as he did his to North Devon. In these hurrying, travelling days, we need to be taught the beauty of " Roots "—

" We see all sights from pole to pole,
And nod, and glance, and hurry by,
And never once possess our souls
Before we die." [2]

Kingsley could have taught us the beauty of actual,

---

[1] " Harzreise."　　　　　　　　　[2] M. Arnold.

as well as of metaphorical, roots; he knew "the secret of the weed's plain heart,"[1] and in a country walk with him we should have made friends with the minutest creatures we passed. Even if we must live in a town, let us read Kingsley's "Town Geology."

> " You cannot rob me of free Nature's grace,
>   You cannot shut the windows of the sky."[2]

To Kingsley these windows were open from his youth up, and the bed-ridden and the sick can see through his eyes, and enter into an inheritance of free Nature's grace, for which our children's children should cherish his memory.

[1] J. R. Lowell.   [2] Thomson's " Castle of Indolence."

II.

" Blessings be with them—and eternal praise,
Who gave us nobler loves and nobler cares—
The Poets, who on earth have made us Heirs
Of truth and pure delight by heavenly lays."

WORDSWORTH.

POETRY should not form the staple of our reading, any more than sugar-plums of our food, but it is very resting and calming to keep some one book of poetry in hand, and read it daily, if only for a few minutes. Mr. Ruskin says that we should be as careful to do this as to read a daily portion of the Bible, that we may be kept in mind of the ideal possibilities of life, and may breathe, for those few moments, a purer atmosphere, in which—

> "The cares that infest the day
> Shall fold their tents like the Arabs
> And as silently steal away." [1]

Many poets soothe and please us by their grace and music, and have no harm in them, except that they are apt to narcotize our moral sense. All poetry that is only pretty, tends to do this; and poetry, even in order to be first-rate poetry, should point to something higher than itself.

Such poets as Wordsworth often seem dull. He himself deprecates a "degrading thirst after

[1] Longfellow.

outrageous stimulation;" and if the literature of his day suggested this to him, what would ours do? If we spend the afternoon reading " idle singers of an empty day,"[1] we run a poorer chance of doing our duty at night; whereas, if we get a few thoughts of Wordsworth into our mind, we are almost sure to take a nobler view of the next question that comes before us.

I hope you possess that old-fashioned thing, a commonplace-book, and that you make constant use of it. Think no time wasted that is spent in copying out really good poetry, the mere act impresses it on your mind, far more than any reading can do.

There are already innumerable books of quotations, and of selected passages for each day in the year, but those that we ourselves collect have a far surpassing value for us. It is very interesting to select a text and a verse of poetry for every day— if the alternate pages of the book are blank, it makes a birthday book, far more satisfactory to the compiler than any printed one. It would be still more interesting to take one virtue for each month, and to bring together the different things said by both poet and prose writers on the subject, though it is hard to find enough quotations on some of the virtues.

It is very interesting to work out a subject in various poets, and to bring together their modes of

[1] Morris's " Earthly Paradise."

treating it, *e.g.* the Poets' Ideal Women, such as Wordsworth's "She was a Phantom of Delight," Lowell's "My Love" and "Irene;" Tennyson's "Isabel;" Milton's "Eve;"[1] Dante's "Beatrice;" Matthew Arnold's "Urania," and many more. Or make a Poets' Garden; flowers would have an added beauty for us if the sight of them brought back to our minds the lines that have turned them into everlastings.

Such a garden might have grass, "not immaculate of the sweet fault of daisies;"[2] out of the grass should spring roses "not royal in their smell alone, but in their hue."[3] There must be a white rose for good Jacobites to wear on June 10th, the Chevalier's birthday (by rights it should be the *rose unique*). There must be "a red red rose that's newly sprung in June" to speak of that other royal exile, Margaret of Anjou. If we are fortunate enough to get it, we must have the old rose of May, *Rose de Meaux*, which Mary Howitt found at Annesley—that most poetical of old houses, a rose which is only seen—

> "Where the great of other days have been;
> Left, like a noble deed, to grace
> The memory of an ancient race."[4]

---

[1] Perhaps Mrs. Catherine Thompson should be considered Milton's Ideal Woman.
[2] George MacDonald.   [3] Ben Jonson.
[4] "Birds and Flowers" (M. Howett).

The border round the grass might be well filled,
even if we restricted ourselves to flowers that bring
us some messages from the past. I have a list of
Chaucerian flowers which would be enough in
itself, and another of Elizabethan ones, which
would require large space. It is curious to notice
what a tidal wave of new flowers came into
England under Queen Elizabeth, not only from
America, but from European countries also, for
the " Art of Simpling," as Gerrard tells us, was
then held "an exercise for the noblest, a pastime
for the best," and many " curious and painfull
Herbalists" in France and Holland were in
correspondence with Gerrard and Parkinson,
helping the one to write his " Herbal," and the
other his " Paradise," which are still the most
fascinating of all flower-books. Elizabeth's nobles
received something more than the instruction in
cricket and football, which we have now agreed to
call a liberal education, and as ambassadors they
had many opportunities of assisting English *savants* ;
Gerrard speaks specially of " the liberalitie of the
Rt. Hon. the Lorde Edward Zouche at his return
from Italy, whence I received many rare seeds
which do flourish in my garden, for which I think
myself much bounde unto his good Lordship." It
would make a garden very interesting if we
collected all the plants mentioned by Bacon in the
essay wherein he directs " the royal ordering of

gardens where there ought to be gardens for all
the months of the year, in which, severally, things
of beauty may be seen in season."

But, even in a town back garden, much may be
done in this way by careful management, while at
least we can pay heed to his reminder that "the
breath of flowers is far sweeter in the air (where it
comes and goes, like the warbling of music) than
in the hand," though we should like also to have
flowers for a true nosegay, or tussiemussie, as
Parkinson calls it. We will so arrange our flowers
as to have a calendar of sweet odours, such as
J. S. Mill drew up for Caroline Fox, not omitting,
as he does, the autumn strawberry leaves, whose
faint smell, according to the old superstition (and
to my Lady Ludlow), can only be discerned by
nostrils of ancient descent!

Under the bedroom window we must have night-
blowing flowers, such as the white rocket—which was
Marie Antoinette's favourite flower, thus bearing
out the old belief that white flowers mean death.
Mignonette, "the fragrant weed, the Frenchman's
darling,"[1] smells sweetest of all, by day and night,
and shall be sown broadcast. Wall-flowers shall
be set, as Lord Bacon would have it, "under the
parlour window;" up the wall shall climb—

> "The fair wild honeysuckle flower
> Seeming of her to speak

---

[1] Cowper's "Task."

Who clings to home—her sheltering bower—
  With loving heart and meek,
  Careless for self, but full of care,
  That home be ever sweet and fair." [1]

But sweet smells shall not be the only creden-
tials to admit flowers to our garden, quaint names
shall be an open sesame, the oxlip daisy shall ride
in triumphantly because " our women," says
Gerrard, " had named them Jacke an apes on
horseback : " " daffodils and the green world they
live in " when brought to us by " March, the first
redresser of the winter's wrong shall be the more
welcome, because Gerrard tells us that " the
Persians do name him the King's chalice." Rose-
campion shall come in with its " clear light-giving
flowers " under its Dutch name of " Christes Eye,"
and the old English one of " Nonsuch." We will
have Crown Imperial, the yellow lily, because,
when George Herbert humbly craved to know,
" sweet peace where dost thou dwell ? " he spied
this gallant flower, and thought—

" Peace at the root must dwell."

But Herbert found he was wrong, and we must
put a royal carpet for this Imperial Crown of the
true Heartsease, with its old pet names of " Cull
me to you," and " Kiss me ere I rise." Ours shall
be the sweet strife—

[1] " Church Poetry " (collected by A. Mozley).

> " Why pansies, eyes that laugh, bear beauty's prize
> From violets, eyes that dream."[1]

And if the old proverb be true—" The Garden is a mute Gospel "—surely violets are its sweetest text ; listen to Gerrard's quaint sermon thereon, which is not yet out of date, though three hundred generation of violets have preached it, since he put it into words for them.

" Gardens receive by these the greatest ornament of all, chiefest beauty, and most gallant grace ; and the recreation of the minde which is taken hereby, cannot but be verie goode and honest : for they admonish and stir up a man to that which is comely and honest; for flowers through their beautie do bring to a liberal and gentlemanlie minde, the remembrance of honestie, comelinesse, and all kinds of virtue. For it would be an unseemely and filthie thing for him that dothe looke upon and handel faire and beautifull things, and who frequenteth and is conversaunt in faire and beautifull places, to have his minde not faire but filthie and deformed."

Flower lovers will forgive this long digression, for they know the temptation of the subject, and perhaps in our climate it is as well for every one to be able to find outdoor pleasures by means of books : all who can, would " go to the woods and hills " to read—

[1] " Paracelsus."

G

"A lesson that will keep
 Their heart from fainting, and their soul from sleep;"[1]

but too often, in default of summer pleasures, we must do as Mr. Lowell did when May proved "a pious fraud of the almanac" ·—

"Warmly walled by books,
 I take my May down from the happy shelf
 Where perch the world's rare song-birds in a row,
 And beg an alms of spring-time, ne'er denied
 Indoors by vernal Chaucer, whose fresh woods
 Throb thick with merle and mavis all the year."[2]

In any words about poetry, I cannot speak too strongly of the importance of learning by heart. If you were blind, or sitting with a sick person in a darkened room, or walking over the moors, you might very likely wish for poetry: would it be at your command? Besides, the best poetry, until you have learnt it by heart, will not yield you all its riches: part is on the surface; but the best is hoarded till you earn it by real effort of memory and will.

An old lady said to me the other day that she had never been educated, but that there was hardly a page of Shakespeare and Milton which her father had not made her study and paraphrase, till she realized every shade of meaning in it. I envied her that "no education," and I fear we are all too busy nowadays with the educational

[1] Longfellow.   [2] "Under the Willows."

advantages showered upon us, to go through such
teaching as that. But I would draw your attention
to smaller poets too, and more especially would
I break a lance for Mrs. Hemans. She has a
delicacy of feeling and expression and a wide range
of subjects which make the present neglect of her,
one of the uncultivating influences of the day.
Inez de Castro, Ivan the Terrible, Alaric, Bernardo
del Carpio, Tasso, Sebastian, Crescentius, Conradin,
were all personal friends to those who in old days
learnt Mrs. Hemans by heart; but I fear that girls,
now, too often find their names non-conductors.
There is a stage in life when we are ashamed to
own allegiance to any poetry so simple as Mrs.
Hemans and Longfellow; we are even half
inclined in those younger days to apologize for
Tennyson himself as being too intelligible. In later
life we gain the courage of our opinions, and hail
such streams as flowing from Parnassus, in spite of
their waters being so clear !

There is a special pleasure in attacking such
poems as Browning's " Easter Eve," and " Paracelsus," but it is the pleasure of hard thought,—a
charm shared with Butler's " Analogy "—and hardly
belonging to them as poetry, though they are
rich in poetical beauties. There is also special
charm about such poetry as George Herbert and
Vaughan, where the thought, though simple, is
so concisely put, that you need to learn much

of it by heart before you realize the fulness of
each line.   Isaac Williams, in " Thoughts for Past
Years," has learnt much of this weightiness, and
many of Archbishop Trench's poems also would
well repay learning by heart, and would prove a
store of strength for the dark hours which he so
well understood.

The mention of religious poetry leads us
necessarily to Keble, though it is to be feared
that the present generation of Church people have
transferred to less sober devotional works, the
study which, thirty years ago, was given to " The
Christian Year."   Perhaps Keble's hope that he
might establish " a sober standard of feeling in
matters of practical religion," is still far from
fulfilment, but yet his words of truth and soberness
have gained a marvellous hold on English Church
people : as Sir John Coleridge points out in his
life of Keble, "a library book, or a book of the
house, is just what it is not ; it is rather a book of
each person, and of each room in the house."
While unlike Wesley's hymns in form, it yet
appeals, like them, with simplicity and directness
to personal religious sentiment, though the reserve,
which is one of its chief characteristics, may
prevent a careless reader from noticing the many
lines in each poem which speak to the inmost
heart.   It may not be one of the least benefits
derived from its study if it teach us to appreciate

the charm of such reserve, rare in this age of autobiographies and *Journals Intimes.*

George MacDonald complains that the poetry of " The Christian Year " is like " Berlin work in iron —hard and delicate," but what can be more touch- ing in its sympathy than the poem on loneliness for the Twenty-fourth Sunday after Trinity, or those for the Monday and Wednesday before Easter ?

Wordsworthian love of Nature is another feature of the book. Principal Shairp points out in his delightful monograph on " Keble and the 'Christian Year,'" that Keble is the only poet who has noticed the singing of the solitary thrush in distant fields, during the hush that preludes the thunderstorm. But it is not only the Oxfordshire and Gloucester- shire scenery so familiar to the poet, that he faithfully describes. Dean Stanley, that most graphic of travellers, has noticed the accuracy of touch with which Keble pictures the Holy Land, as in the poems for the Third Sundays in Advent and Lent. As Keble never went to Palestine, this shows not only his quick insight into nature, but also his close study of the hints to be found in the Bible and in modern travels. Minute knowledge of the Bible is noticeable in every page of his book ; it needs special observation on the reader's part, to detect the extent to which the poems are imbued with scriptural thoughts and expressions. A clergyman in a rural part of Worcestershire was in the habit of reading the poem for the Sunday, and explaining it from the pulpit, in lieu of an afternoon sermon. Many may feel, though the poems often contain an excellent skeleton of a sermon, yet that they would be only suitable to a bookish congregation, and to one of a peculiar school of thought; but those to whom "The Christian Year" is a household word, feel rather, "all the lore its scholars need," is "pure eyes and Christian hearts," and that, though it is a watchword of a special school, yet its spirit is truly that of Christ's Universal Church.

Perhaps the poem on S. Matthew's Day is Keble's high-water mark of poetry. This and the sonnet on Westminster Bridge are the two poems which most perfectly express the poetry of the town—both given us by men who keenly felt the inspiration of the country.[1]

"The Christian Year" is strongly marked by scholarly and patristic learning; but we hardly pause to consider such points in a book which so belongs to our devotions, and so colours our Bible reading.

Can we ever picture to ourselves, except in Keble's setting, such scenes as Balaam on Peor, Joshua's Conquest, the Feeding of the Five Thousand, Elijah on Mount Horeb, Ezekiel's Vision, the Three Holy Children?

[1] For this thought I am indebted to Miss Wordsworth.

Are we ever in the mountains without learning from Keble to hear—

"Such sounds as make deep silence in the heart
For Thought to do her part"?

Can the year close without the thought of the line (and all that follows it)—

" Will God indeed with fragments bear ? "

St. John, St. Philip, and St. James, St. Barnabas and St. Matthew all speak to us in Keble's words :—his lines on the Catechism and the Burial of the Dead, and the morning and evening hymns are in themselves enough to give him almost as unquestioned a place in our religious life as the Prayer Book itself.

Surely no other uninspired writer has so grown into the very fibre of the religious life of a nation.

A Shadow from the Merchant of Venice.

ANTONIO is a spirit "finely touched!" so finely that to say he was a gentleman is too coarse a definition for so fine a nature—he would shiver in hearing it said of him—as Bassanio *should* have done, in saying it of himself.

But, roughly speaking, that is what Shakespeare makes him in every touch, emphasizing it by contrast with Bassanio. Bassanio is, at first sight, such a fine young fellow—a frank-hearted soldier, a free-handed young noble, whose qualities are just such as to impress Nerissa, and, alas! her mistress also. What a pity Portia was not raised to her best self by marrying Antonio, for Bassanio would have been equally happy with Nerissa.

Surely Shakespeare must himself have been very like Antonio, to be able to draw with such delicate touches the commonness of Bassanio's real nature. He makes us feel the charm of the young fellow; one hardly wonders that Antonio loves him—he must, many a time, have brought sunshine to the older man, and this, partly through his very inability to understand the moods in which Antonio

wearied of his own sadness. He had a childlike
trust in the sympathy of Antonio (from whose love
he " had a warranty to unburden all his plots and
purposes ") which must have endeared him to the
more reserved nature, to whom such trust in
another's sympathy would have meant far more
than Bassanio could have possibly understood.

If Antonio could ever have got near enough
to such a woman as * * * he too might have
" truly grown a talker "—unless she had understood
without words, as the little mermaid would have
done. But I greatly doubt if he could have
married ; he had an ideal woman in his mind,
something like his mother, of an older generation,
and whom he had never met in life ; and he
never found out that with an understanding wife
by his side he might have been twice the man he
was.

Who should that wife have been ? Mary Collet
and Romola would not have roused him enough
on his dark days. Realmah's Ainah would have
made him happy, but I am inclined to think that
Miss Edgeworth's Lady Geraldine, in " Ennui,"
would have been the best match for him,—she
would have made him not only happy, but
successful.

In his own circle I can find no wife for him :
Portia would never have had patience with a man
so apt, when anything jarred on him, to shrink

silently back into himself, rather than follow it out in words and questions. She would have exchanged gossip with Solanio, while Antonio discussed politics with Salarino. She has wit, but not wisdom; she is merely clever, her nature is not deep enough to be wise. But she is worldly-wise: she has watched the fate of the wives of "spunges,"—she is business-like in the trial,—she has the ready tact of a practised hostess when she tells Morocco that he stands "as fair as any comer she has looked on yet." Nothing escapes her, and she probably could draw as good caricatures with her pencil as with her tongue. But her want of reserve jars on us; not only does she chatter more freely to Nerissa than Beatrice and Hero do to their waiting women, but she even "chaffs" the servant who bring news of Bassanio's courier. She speaks of Bassanio before he comes, in a way that quite harmonizes with her having conveyed to him "fair speechless messages" on his earlier visit.

Notice by the way, that both mistress and maid are wooed in much the same way,—by much the same kind of man. Bassanio would have been equally happy with Nerissa, while there is just so much of finer touch in Portia, as forbids our mating her with Gratiano, and sets us wondering whether she might not have been raised by marriage with Antonio. But doubtless, Fate, which was kind to Bassanio in giving him his heart's desires, was ever kinder to Antonio, in saving him from a happiness which would have made him a smaller man. He was better left with the "shadow's bliss" of an empty house.

Did he ever stay at Belmont? I doubt it!—at least, not after the first few months. Portia, who had so fallen in love with Bassanio's "presence," that he was, for the time, her highest ideal (on hearing of Antonio's perfections, she felt he "must be like my lord")—this same Portia will soon see the flaws in the handsome "jolly" adventurer, who, in honour of Antonio's first visit to the pair, at Belmont, will take too much wine at dinner on the night of his arrival. When they rejoin Portia, she will see Bassanio in his stupid good-humoured stage,—she will see him through the eyes of Antonio, the grave, thoughtful, Venetian *grand seigneur.*

Surely the woman, who could speak with such heart and brain in the Doge's Palace, will feel, after a few such evenings, that she is worthy of something better than Fate has given her; and she will hate the man who unconsciously opened her eyes, and who will be credited by her, with far more criticism of her husband than he is really guilty of. Besides, I am afraid Antonio *will* grow critical; his incipient resenting of Portia (shown in his impatient remark about "thy wife's command-ment") will open his eyes to the real Bassanio more than any of the latter's early escapades has done.   He will probably grow to like Portia the best of the two, unless, indeed, he comes to think that the married Bassanio has developed feet of clay through his wife's influence, instead of having had them all along !

But all this is a digression, for we were busily discussing whether marriage would have made Antonio "grow a talker."   As it was, he truly describes himself when he says, "I am dumb." For he *was* dumb, both in fewness of words, and still more so as regarded expression of the deeper side of his nature.

He says most, in the opening scene, to Salarino, who cares for him, as *he* cared for Bassanio.   But this is not altogether an instance in point, since it is not entirely a momentary impulse of confidence in Salarino, but is also a part of his one weakness —the *défaut* of his *qualité,*—a weakness of melancholy which is, perhaps, a part of his finer nature. Mr. Ruskin says that a sense of " O the pity of it," is the constant underlying feeling of the true gentleman's outlook on the world ; but, in Antonio, this is apt to degenerate into self-pity, he is too ready to feel himself "the tainted wether of the flock ; " a sojourn at " Abu Telfan," to teach him what real sorrow meant, would have strengthened his nature.

Abu Telfan may not be marked on the moral

maps of my readers, so I had better explain that, many years ago, a certain German, whose adventures were written by Raabe, was taken prisoner by an African tribe, and given as slave to an old negress in the village of Abu Telfan. Here he went through such deep waters of cruelty and degradation that on his eventual rescue and return to Berlin, all subsequent misfortunes seemed to him as mere jesting on the part of fate. Abu Telfan has suburbs in every country under the sun, and the initiated who have sojourned there (and yet kept a stout heart) may be known by a certain serenity of temper which sometimes causes them to be confounded (only by the uninitiated) with those who are serene merely because life has not yet crossed them.

In one place Antonio gives utterance to the poetry that, at other times, he locks up in his own heart. When confronted with death, he shows a power of words which betray his underlying nature doubly :—first, as proving him a poet (a poet who may have written but would never have published), and next, as showing what a shock, to his sensitive nature, was the approach of death. Only supreme excitement would have unloosed his tongue, and a less imaginative, coarser nature might have faced death with far less nervous strain, and so perhaps have felt more heroic. Antonio was probably physically a coward, because he realized things. In a minor degree this power of realization comes out in his sensitive perception of the picture which he himself will make—" Say how I loved you, speak me fair in death." Here is the cultivated and complex Venetian temperament, unlike the simple heroism of an English—of a northern—nature. The most simple and direct of all his feelings is his love for Bassanio, the sweet-natured harum-scarum boy, whom he had doubtless helped out of a hundred scrapes—helped so often that he had weakened the boy's proper pride ; it is hardly Bassanio's fault that he is so ready to ask Antonio for more money. How ready he is to listen to the boy's story ! " Tell me now of the lady "—(was it perhaps a shock to Antonio, unexpressed even to himself, that money difficulties came first to the young fellow's tongue, instead of the love story which Antonio expected ?) —" he only loved the world for him." How ready, in Bassanio's trouble, is the offer of Antonio's purse and person ! When trouble came to himself, Antonio cared not, " if only Bassanio came " to show the answering love, which he probably very often forgot to give. Bassanio must unconsciously have wounded his friend a dozen times a day. How much, do you suppose, was conveyed to *him* by Antonio's reproach : " You wrong my love by questioning it ! " ?

The more I watch those two together, the more

I wonder at Antonio's infatuation, unless indeed, as some one suggested to me, Antonio had been in love with Bassanio's mother. Bassanio is " the average Englishman who remains, if not a school-boy, an undergraduate." Antonio was, what is rare in every nation, a full-grown and thoughtful man. But, after all, why should their unlikeness be a difficulty? Are friends alike, as Portia thought? Antonio, " being the bosom lover of her lord," must he needs be like him?

Who are Antonio's brothers-in-arms in the better world where, as Swedenborg held, likeness of soul is the only means of meeting? Surely Charles I., Don Quixote, Dante, Sir Philip Sidney, Lord Falkland, George Herbert, John Inglesant, Sir Richard Grenville, Sir Ralph Verney, are now his friends.

> "There do the band, that now in triumph shines
> And that (before they were invested thus)
> In earthly bodies carried heavenly minds,
> Pitch round about, in order glorious,
> Their sunny tents and houses luminous,
> And from their eyes joy looks, and laughs at pain."[1]

The only sister souls I can think of, to join this band, are Antigone and Lucy Hutchinson, though, having great faith in education, I am inclined to think that if Lady Macbeth had had better influences around her in early life, and had married differently, she might have been fit for this

[1] Giles Fletcher.

constellation of "fair women;" but then, it is only the over-education of Hypatia which renders *her* unworthy of a place, so the education must be carefully administered.

Perhaps the difficulty lies in the fact that the highest kind of woman, as well as the happiest, is she "who has no history," and so perhaps some, of whom least is said, are most closely related to these "solitary hearted" ones. Such are, Jephthah's daughter, Ruth, Judith, and Esther; it is only for a moment that we see them, but, if we may judge them by that moment, they are "Queens of noble Nature's crowning." [1]

Whether fit or not for Antonio and his noble company, they are far above Bassanio, with his reliance on Portia's appreciation of himself; the chivalry of "I that loved and you that liked" would never have dawned upon him, though I feel sure it was a favourite song of Antonio's. When he describes Portia, he only dwells on her locks, her *eyes* say nothing to him except when "therein he sees himself." His description of her portrait in the casket scene, is the studio jargon of the young Venetian, accustomed to haunt his friends' studios, and criticize their models. It is the surface admiration to be expected of the man who is hail-fellow-well-met with every one, and enjoys the horse-play of Gratiano. "*Il y a quelque chose*

[1] Hartley Coleridge.

le pire que le manque de goût," said Victor Hugo, "*c'est le manque de dégoût;*" any sort of company pleases Bassanio, even Shylock is asked to dinner (though *he* has the good taste to refuse—the *manque de dégoût* is the last fault with which one can charge Shylock !).

This same want of true pride comes out in his spending more than he has, and in his readiness to ask Antonio for more money. His false pride comes out in his " rich liveries "—his " gifts of rich value " (all paid for by Antonio) ; in his thinking money can settle all debts, the " courteous pains " of the young advocate included. (Antonio feels that they are " indebted to him in love and service evermore," over and above the 3,000 ducats.) This same Bassanio is quick in assuming his ownership at Belmont, the " youth of his new interest " is a second thought when he welcomes Lorenzo and Salarino.

Nerissa calls him a scholar, and he has school-boy tags of quotation, which he uses to Antonio in Act I., but they come out again in the casket scene, so we may conclude they had done duty already on his first visit, and impressed Portia and Nerissa. In the casket scene we find Portia talking up to the classical level of " her lord "—she will know better by-and-by !

Learning was fashionable among the young Venetians—Jacopo Foscari was probably not

H

alone in his fondness for Greek books; and there
were plenty of young nobles who enjoyed literary
talk with Petrarch when he was at Venice, more
than a hundred years before. Bassanio was quick
enough to catch the colouring of his day, and he
was helped by a gift of words. His ready give
and take with Portia, at a supreme moment of his
life, suggest a good diner-out in calmer circumstances.

When he was " giddy in spirit, gazing in a doubt,"
have we a touch of the self-questioning, self-disgust,
which probably came to Antonio in most moments
of success ?—Or was it merely astonishment at his
luck ? Perhaps Portia read it in a way that
quickened her own humility seen in the answering
speech—and there only !

But, after all, these various instances of *manque de
goût*, and *manque de dégoût*, are but minor matters
compared to the want of principle in this adventurer; for, though a noble by accident, Bassanio
was a mere adventurer by nature.

Not to serve Bassanio himself, would Antonio
have pleaded with any Judge, " to do a little
wrong ; "—and Portia spoke a truer word in jest
than would have pleased her had she understood
it, when she said he " knew not his own honour "
in keeping the ring. Bassanio said " his honour
would not let ingratitude so much besmear it," as
to refuse the ring ; but had Antonio " riveted a ring

with faith unto *his* flesh," he would not have "plucked it from his finger," for any argument of false generosity,—had even Portia in her own person prayed for it, he would have taught her that he "loved honour more."

DOUBTLESS many have tried to read Words-worth and given up in despair, feeling quite unable to care for him; but, as we know that those whose judgment is far better than our own, love and value him, let us determine to learn his secret and to go on reading and learning till our eyes are opened. Many can tell us from experience how far more than repaid we shall be, if we persevere. There is not much incident in his life, only the development of the soul; but, as Browning says, little else is worth study.

Three things must be remembered, if we are to understand him — the country he lived in, the times he lived in, and the friends he lived with.

He was born in Cumberland and passed his boyhood there, returning to the north when he was twenty-nine, to spend his manhood at Gras-mere, in Westmoreland. Surely no country has ever found expression so perfectly as the Lake Country did in Wordsworth's poetry. He under-stood and gave voice to "the souls of lonely places," while, in return, no other poet has owed

so much to the country round him. Mr. Pater
says, that to read one of his long pastoral poems
for the first time, is like taking a walk in a new
country. No other poet gives such wonderfully
precise and vivid pictures in a single line.

> " The pliant hare-bell swinging in the breeze
>   On some grey rock."
> " The single sheep and the one blasted tree
>   And the bleak music from that old stone wall."
> " And that green corn all day is rustling in thine ears."

The first fact to note in Wordsworth's life is,
that he was, heart and soul, and eyes and ears, a
Northcountryman. The second is, that he lived in
the days of the French Revolution. Liberty, and
the Brotherhood of Man, formed the great Gospel
of that day ;—the new wine which got put into the
wrong bottles, but which was heavenly wine all the
same. We shall see traces of this in some of
the best poetry of Wordsworth, who travelled in
France during the hopeful days of the Revolution,
landing at Calais in 1789, on the day when trees of
Liberty were planted all over France. He was
nineteen, and—

> " To be young was very Heaven.
>   A glorious time
>   A happy time that was : triumphant looks
>   Were then the common language of all eyes."

He was an ardent Radical in those days—a

believer in progress — but the course of the
Revolution destroyed his hope and faith in
human nature, till life among stalwart Cumbrian
statesmen and shepherds restored it.   The per-
sistent believers in revolution looked on him as a
backslider when he joined the party of Law and
Order and Conservatism; — Browning's "Lost
Leader" is supposed to refer to Wordsworth's
accepting the office of Poet Laureate, since the
latter's earlier Republican views would have made
him scorn to receive any gift from a king.

Thus, between twenty and thirty (generally the
" *Sturm und Drang*" period of a man's life—the
unsettled, rebellious stage), the world was out of
joint for him.   But he learnt to "see into the life
of things," and to find an Eternal Law in Nature,
the thought of which was a sheet anchor to him,
when human goodness and beauty seemed to
crumble away.

He was also helped by the third great factor of
his life—his friends.   Chief of them was Dorothy
Wordsworth, his sister, who came to live with him
when he was twenty-five.—("She gave me eyes, she
gave me ears.")—He read much of his poetry in
"the shooting lights of her wild eyes," and her
diary has the first hint of many a poem of his—
e.g. "Calais Sands," "Westminster Bridge,"
"Daffodils."

His other friend was Coleridge, whom he always

thought the most wonderful man he ever knew. In 1797, Coleridge visited the brother and sister at Alfoxden in Somerset, and here they planned " Lyrical Ballads," an epoch-making book, which contained "The Ancient Mariner," " The Tables Turned," " Expostulation and Reply," and " Tintern Abbey."

These poems struck an entirely new note in poetry :—if Wordsworth had died then, he would have been one of the few voices in this world of echoes. Not only was the insight into nature new, but the very language was new. To us it seems natural that a poet should express himself clearly and simply, but this is a new order of things, which we owe to Wordsworth. When you rebel against the over-plainness, the doggrel, of some of his poems, you must remember that he was a crusader in behalf of the truth to nature which could touch men's hearts; and that he was fighting against shams and unreality, which were eating the life out of poetry.

We may say that Wordsworth's education lasted till the age of thirty, when he settled finally into his northcountry life at Grasmere. The first period includes his early Cumbrian school, King's College, Cambridge, his travels in France, his life in Somerset, and a final year at Goslar near Hamburg, where some of his finest, most delicate work was done, *e.g.* " Lucy Gray," " Ruth," " Nutting,"

"The Poet's Epitaph," "Lucy." (With the restrained, silent passion of this last, compare those lines in which Browning touches almost his high-water mark of feeling : " But cannot praise, I love so much.")

At Goslar he also planned the " Prelude," which was not finished for six years, and only published after his death. It is an epic poem on his own education, a history of his own mind. Read it carelessly, and you will find it intolerably dull :— read it to mark any beautiful line you can discover, and you will be surprised to find how much you will mark, and you will love the bits all the more for having discovered them :—notice, too, how few men could remain so great while chronicling such small things.

We now come to the inspired decade of Words-worth's life, 1798-1808. The outward incidents were : 1799, life at Grasmere ; 1800, friendship with Lamb ; 1802, marriage with Mary Hutchinson ; 1803, his tour in Scotland and the Napoleonic War, with Nelson as its hero. Wordsworth's inner life showed itself in the " Four Sonnets on Personal Talk," " There is an Eminence," " Daffodils ; " 1803, " Highland Girl," " Stepping Westward," " The Solitary Reaper," " Yarrow Unvisited ; " 1805, Sonnets (on " Venice," " Toussaint," " Two Voices," " O Friend," " Milton," " A Roman Master ") and the " Happy Warrior," our most permanent literary record of the Napoleonic War; 1806, "Odes to Duty and Immortality."

For another ten years he was still a poet, though a lesser one. We get, in 1815, "The White Doe," setting forth "purification as the joy of pain;" and after this he writes only verse, not poetry, with such occasional flashes as we find in "Ecclesiastical Sonnets," 1822. He lives on for thirty years longer, and in 1843 succeeds Southey as Poet Laureate :—to be succeeded in his turn by Tennyson, who received in 1850—

> "This laurel greener from the brows
> Of him that uttered nothing base."

What is Wordsworth's position in English poetry? Matthew Arnold ranks him next to the four great modern poets, Shakespeare, Milton, Goethe, and Molière. He was "a morning star of song,"[1] one of a group of six, who gave us our present poetry, the others being Coleridge, Scott, Byron, Keats, Shelley, who were all helpers in the cause Wordsworth had so much at heart—the superseding Pope's artificiality by the language of Nature.

Wordsworth and Coleridge were critics as well as poets, and have left their reasons for thus writing. Wordsworth, in his preface to "Lyrical Ballads," contends that the peasantry alone speak straight to the heart, and that poetry and prose

[1] "Vision of Poets," by E. B. B.

should use the same diction, *i.e.* he was so provoked with the misuse of poetical diction that he wanted to discard it altogether.

Coleridge was wiser; he agreed with Wordsworth in trying to bring in a language of natural sense and feeling, but he held that educated men, like Hooker and Spenser, could speak as straight to the heart as the peasantry, and play upon more strings in it. Also he held that poetry represents warmer emotions than prose, and therefore should have its own appropriate diction.

Wordsworth was so true a poet, that he could not help (in spite of his theories) writing in this finer, truer language. His strongest work is in his lyrics, such as "The Cuckoo," "The Reaper," "The Fountain;" and in such sonnets as "Westminster Bridge." The style and expression in these is admitted by all judges to be unique in its perfection : " They have set a standard of pure and sincere diction in poetry, as Cardinal Newman has done in prose—both these men have shown us unsuspected powers in the English language." [1]

Wordsworth has his own style, (as parodies can testify). There is a famous piece about " The Boy on Winander," of which Lamb said, "Had I had met those lines running wild in the deserts of Arabia, I should have shrieked out ' Wordsworth ! ' "

[1] Matthew Arnold.

There are minor points we should notice in reading Wordsworth, before we go on to the real reasons for the reverence which is now shown him by the finest judges. One is his wonderful perception of sound. Only Wordsworth would have felt "that beauty born of murmuring sound would pass into a face." The next is, that he prefers "the short and simple annals of the poor"[1] to Scott's feudal lords : many have since taught us to see that the House Beautiful stands by the wayside, that Love and Sorrow and Self-sacrifice are no respecters of persons ; but it was a new idea in Wordsworth's day, and was partly the cause of Jeffery's famous criticism in the *Edinburgh Review* on " The Excursion,"—" This will never do ! " Certainly " The Excursion " is dull. Mr. Lowell says every long poem, except the " Odyssey," *is* dull ; but it is a poor thing to pick out the flaws in the work of a man who could truly give the following as the aim of his long life of poetic work : " To console the afflicted ; *to add sunshine to daylight, by making the happy happier ;* to teach the young and gracious of every age, *to see, to think, and feel.*"

This brings us to Matthew Arnold's reasons for his high estimate of Wordsworth. First, the unique quantity of first-class work. Take only two or three bits, and Coleridge, Shelley, and others will be close rivals to him ; but what other poet,

[1] Gray's " Elegy."

when his feebler work has been cleared away, is left with such a mass of genuine poetry. And what is the strength of this first-rate work ? It is that Wordsworth has more to say than any other poet on that which most concerns us—*how to live.* Epictetus compares the pleasant accessories of life and art—form, finish, etc.—to an inn; while " the best and master thing" is *how to live.*

" ' This inn is pleasant.' Yes ! But we are to pass through it, and not to live there. Some poets stay at a pleasant and lovely inn : Wordsworth never does. He helps us to live our best and highest life ; he is a strengthening and purifying influence like his own mountains. Groping in the dark passages of life, we come on some axiom of his, that like a wall, gives us our bearing and enables us to find an outlet."[1] He has the true Teutonic nature which never rests in beauty only, which always turns to the ethical side of things. His is never merely poetry—he always turns our mind to some question of right living. He aimed at being a teacher before all things. Let us make him part of our Sunday reading,—let us mark all the bits which help us to feel as we should aspire to feel—the bits which express what we *do* feel in our best moments : let us go to him as a teacher, and we shall learn to love him as a poet.

[1] Matthew Arnold.

Some poets remind us of the lines—

> " She's like the keystone of an arch
> That consummates all beauty:
> She's like the music of a march
> That sheds a joy on Duty."

Wordsworth is like this, in that he does not merely set our lives to music, which is the Poet's mission;—he is not only the music to a march, but he makes us march,—which is the Teacher's mission.

In the hurry and bustle of this life, he makes us hear the sound of many voices underlying it, and reminds us that there is something nobler and more permanent in life, than the petty selfish interests and pleasures, which tend to absorb us; he reminds us of the Eternal Laws which underlie life, and are the only reality.

He is pre-eminently a poet who helps to make us dutiful: let us constrain ourselves to read him, and we shall—

> " When we have parted up the hill
> Of Duty with reluctant will,
> Be thankful, even though tired and faint,
> For the rich bounties of constraint."

" The Happy Warrior."

" There is no portrait fitter than that of the Happy Warrior to go forth to all lands as representing the English character at its height—a figure not ill-matching with ' Plutarch's men.' "—F. W. MYERS.

" WHO is the happy Warrior? Who is he
    That every man in arms should wish to be?"

Wordsworth answers his own question by drawing a picture which has been called "a summary of patriotism, a manual of national honour." Read —or, better still, learn by heart—this poem inspired by Nelson, our great sailor, and Tennyson's ode on our great soldier, the Duke of Wellington, and you will know what " England expects " of her sons.

" Who is the happy Warrior? . . .
    It is the generous Spirit, who, when brought
    Among the tasks of real life, hath wrought
    Upon the plan that pleased his boyish thought."

Generous, in the ordinary acceptation of the word, is hardly the term we should apply to the prudent deliberate nature described in the poem, but in the original sense of " well born " it suggests to us one

who has been surrounded by ennobling influences
from the very first.

> " Whose high endeavours are an inward light
> That makes the path before him always bright."

As a boy he appreciates the true aim and
methods of education.

> " Who, with natural instinct to discern
> What knowledge can perform, is diligent to learn,
> Abides by this resolve, and stops not there,
> But makes his moral being his prime care."

He sees that the soul must come first and the mind
second, if the mind itself is to be fully developed.
A great educationalist once said, " Teach a boy
arithmetic only and let me teach another boy both
arithmetic and religion : other things being equal,
the second boy will beat the first in arithmetic."
Develop the whole nature, and each separate
faculty will stand a better chance.

So far we have had the Happy Warrior's education, now we see its result when he goes into the
world.

> " Who, doomed to go in company with Pain,
> And Fear, and Bloodshed, miserable train !
> Turns his necessity to glorious gain ;
> In face of these doth exercise a power
> Which is our human nature's highest dower ;
> Controls them and subdues, transmutes, bereaves
> Of their bad influence, and their good receives."

The well trained, well disciplined nature is King over Circumstances, and experiences, as every growing nature does, the advantage of disadvantages.

Wordsworth goes on to give instances of this power of transmuting base metal into gold—

> " By objects, which might force the soul to abate
> Her feeling, rendered more compassionate ;
> Is placable—because occasions rise
> So often that demand such sacrifice ;
> More skilful in self-knowledge, even more pure
> As tempted more ; more able to endure
> As more exposed to suffering and distress ;
> Thence also, more alive to tenderness."

He does well to put " tenderness " as the culminating point. Many natures learn from suffering, endurance, and purity of self-control, but they are apt to demand of others the strength they have themselves shown. It means a rare and beautiful nature when "out of the strong comes forth sweetness."

We now find the keynote of the Happy Warrior's character—

> " 'Tis he whose law is reason ; who depends
> Upon that law as on the best of friends."

He and Cordelia are brother and sister,—(I will not say husband and wife, for two such eminently reasonable people would hardly have attracted each other !)

There was no statecraft about the Happy Warrior, no expediency, no opportunism, no compromise, no putting up with a low standard, because he was obliged to work with imperfect instruments.

> " Whence, in a state where men are tempted still
> To evil for a guard against worse ill,
> And what in quality or act is best
> Doth seldom on a right foundation rest,
> He labours good on good to fix, and owes
> To virtue every triumph that he knows."

Whether as a chairman of a committee or as a prime minister, he would have said, like the great duke, " I haven't time not to do right."

In public life the question sometimes comes, Is a man to throw up office and, presumably, harm his party because of personal scruples ? Is he to bring a private standard of honour into public life? Wordsworth says " Yes," and suggests that the politician helps the nation more by keeping up its standard, than by keeping a clever head in office,— his brains are not necessary to God's cause, but his principle is.

> " Who, if he rise to station of command,
> Rises by open means ; and there will stand
> On honourable terms, or else retire,
> And in himself possess his own desire."

The Warrior's whole character is then summed up in two lines—

> "Who comprehends his trust, and to the same
> Keeps faithful with a singleness of aim:"

What is this trust—what special gift has been confided to him? Is it not the moral insight, the realization of the true proportion and value of earthly things, which was his instinct in boyhood? He sees earth in the light of eternity, as Lazarus did in " The Epistle of Karshish," hence—

> "He does not stoop nor lie in wait
> For wealth, or honours, or for worldly state;
> Whom they must follow; on whose head must fall
> Like showers of manna, if they come at all."

He is one of the poor in spirit, who sit loose to the good things of this world. He knows how to abound, but he has the grace of poverty, of detachment, and can suffer need without any change in his inner self.

> " Whose powers shed round him in the common strife,
> Or mild concerns of ordinary life,
> A constant influence, a peculiar grace."

He lives ordinary life on the highest level, and is rewarded by almost unknown powers being developed at a crisis, the exercising of which brings the keen joy of action, which is the spiritualization of the Berserker love of battle.

" But who, if he be called upon to face
Some awful moment to which Heaven has joined
Great issues, good or bad for human kind,
Is happy as a Lover ; and attired
With sudden brightness, like a man inspired."

In that " awful moment " he has the exhilaration
of at last finding full scope for the faculties which
he had contentedly devoted to the day of small
things : at last the world is big enough for him,
and he can stretch his wings. As the powers
which culminate in this inspiration were nursed by
the discipline of obedience, he is rewarded by being
enabled to preserve what seems incompatible with
such rapture, perfect self-control ; he preserves
undimmed the insight of his calmer hours,—

" And through the heat of conflict, keeps the law
In calmness made, and sees what he foresaw."

Here, in the few moments which completely
express his real self, is his one point of contact
with emotion—the strength and insight of reason
are joined with the warmth and force of impulse :
perhaps there is here a glimpse, a suggestion, of
what he will be in a higher life. Till that higher
life comes, he mainly walks on one leg—*i.e.* Reason.
Perhaps it is the best foot to put foremost ; but a
complete man has two ! The description of his
bearing when the crisis comes, enforces the idea

that the "reward of performing one duty is the power to fulfil another."[1]

> "Who, if an unexpected call succeed,
>   Come when it will, is equal to the need."

Then comes a race-touch : a Frenchman would love to "ride in the whirlwind and direct the storm;"[2] a German would prefer to remain undisturbed at the domestic hearth ; the Englishman is equally at home in either life—being the inheritor of the Roman type—the hero that could save the State and then retire again to his cabbages.

> "He who, though thus endued as with a sense
>   And faculty for storm and turbulence,
>   Is yet a Soul whose master-bias leans
>   To home-felt pleasures and to gentle scenes ;
>   Sweet images ! which, wheresoe'er he be,
>   Are at his heart ; and such fidelity
>   It is his darling passion to approve ;
>   More brave for this, that he hath much to love."

He commands better in the field—speaks better in the House—because he, all the time, feels as if he were winning his spurs under his wife's eyes ; he is "approving" himself to her, and is therefore more brave ; the sense of the one public opinion which he does care for, is always at his heart.

The close of this poem reminds us of the picture of his boyhood, and shows us a consistent, a continuous life.

---

[1] George Eliot.   [2] Addison's "Campaign."

"'Tis, finally, the Man, who, lifted high,
Conspicuous object in a Nation's eye,
Or left unthought of in obscurity—
Who, with a toward or untoward lot,
Prosperous or adverse, to his wish or not,
Plays, in the many games of life, that one
Where what he most doth value must be won."

He is Cromwell's ideal Ironside—"what he most doth value" is the acting on principle which we saw in his political career. "Give me a man that hath principle," said Cromwell; "I know where to have him,"—*i.e.* you always know which game of life he will be playing at. He has—what is daily growing a rarer possession—a standard!

"Whom neither shape of danger can dismay,
Nor thought of tender happiness betray:"

To say he does not flinch for either fear or favour seems almost too obvious a trait of strength to be worthy of the more suggestive features which precede it—and yet it is the one intimation that he had the fighting courage of a soldier. The preceding parts show us more the moral courage of the director and statesman.

We saw the *power of growth*, which makes the difference between man and man, in his boyhood's high endeavours and diligence to learn.

"Who not content that former worth stand fast
Looks forward persevering to the last,
From well to better, daily self-surpassed."

Next to reasonableness (we may almost say "sweet

reasonableness "), this power of growth is perhaps the strongest feature in his character.   In later life we see that it needs no competition with others, no rivalry to inspire it with energy,—the seed of worldliness is always lurking in competition, and the Happy Warrior is pre-eminently an unworldly man.

> " Who, whether praise of him must walk the earth
> For ever, and to noble deeds give birth,
> Or he must go to dust without his fame,
> And leave a dead unprofitable name—
> Finds comfort in himself and in his cause."

What has been "his cause" all through his life ? Is it not " what he most doth value,"—" his trust " —*i.e.* the triumph of principle ?   His life and aims are based on Reality—he has touched the Rock—and can never suddenly awake to feel his life a failure and his aim misplaced.   Whether he die early or late he "can never mourn a head grown grey, a heart grown cold *in vain.*"   He finds comfort "in himself"—*i.e.* in his sense of progress—he feels he is not standing still : the fact of his being daily self-surpassed makes life worth living.

We must own that, from first to last, in the Happy Warrior, there is no touch of the sense of sin, there is a Pagan serenity and completeness in his life.   He is of the family of John the Baptist,

¹ Shelley's " Adonais."

and the least in the Kingdom of Heaven is greater
than he. The imperfection of the saints, compared
to the Happy Warrior, " is precisely because of
their wider nature."

> " He, while the mortal mist is gathering, draws
> His breath in confidence of Heaven's applause."

Even while allowing for the limitation which
runs through the whole character, this word
"applause" grates on our ears; we feel that the
Happy Warrior's ideal must have been small indeed
if applause, in the ordinary sense of the word,
could have been grateful to his ears. We must
keep to the stricter sense of " approval," such as
that which Hildebrand would have looked for
when he said he had loved righteousness and
hated iniquity. The Happy Warrior had a right
to feel that he had been on God's side all through
the battle of life ; he may well feel that, much as he
may have failed in execution, only in Heaven will
his aims be sympathized with and approved. His
deep nature, marked by inward gravity of soul (by
the "moral thoughtfulness" which Arnold desired
to see in his Sixth), must always have felt more or
less of a stranger and pilgrim among the shallower
natures around him,—it can hardly have been
earthly joy which made him the *Happy* Warrior
" that every man in arms should wish to be."

IT is related of a Chinese ambassador to this country that he desired to see some poets : accordingly, he and his interpreter were sent to call on Mr. Browning. The latter, knowing that his guest was himself a poet, inquired whether his writings were lyrical, dramatic, or pastoral, to which the interpreter replied that His Excellency's poetry was chiefly enigmatical. That two of a trade met on this occasion, must be allowed by the warmest of Mr. Browning's admirers; but where they join issue with the world at large, is in saying that that labour is well bestowed in searching for *le mot de l'énigme.* The denouncers of Mr. Browning's obscurity are mostly those who have never given him more than a cursory reading, and from that they cannot expect much result, seeing that Coleridge used to say of the plainest book ever written, " The Pilgrim's Progress," that he read it three times : first, as a theologian ; second, with devotional feelings ; third, as a poet. Surely, we should bestow at least as much study on a

confessedly [1] obscure style, before dismissing it as
unfathomable.   In saying this, it is, of course, taken
for granted that the subject-matter is worthy of
being studied, and few thoughtful persons who have
fairly considered the question will refuse to grant
so much to Browning.   In this very poem of
" Paracelsus," though there are many beauties that
he who runs may read, yet a large number of people
shrink from the mental labour involved in grappling
with it as a whole, and say of the prophet of our
day, as those of old did of Ezekiel—" Doth he not
speak parables?"   The following sketch of the
poem is intended, in a very slight degree, to aid
such as are unaccustomed to Browning's style, to
read it for themselves.

Like almost all his works, it deals with ' the incidents in the development of a soul;" he says
himself that he considers "little else worth study,"
and, by looking at all incidents in this light of
soul-growth, he reads lofty spiritual life into the
minutest trait of character; in Browning's eyes man
can " nothing common do or mean," [2] because there
is a deep significance in all his words and deeds,
since "in the mental, as in the bodily organism,
the present is the resultant of the past, so that whatever we learn, think, or do, will come again in later

[1] "To bring the invisible full into play,
   Let the visible go to the dogs—what matter?"
[2] Andrew Marvell.

life as a Nemesis, or as an angel's visit."[1] He inter-
weaves time and eternity; teaching us that, it may
be, our life will be continuous, "forever old, yet
new; changed not in kind, but in degree," and that
" Eternity is not to be railed off from time, as if *that*
were the High Altar, and *this* the profane street."[1]

The poem opens A.D. 1512, in a garden near
Würzburg, where Paracelsus, an ambitious lad
of nineteen, is bidding farewell to his friend Festus,
and to Michál, the latter's bride, telling them that
their memories shall make his heart "quiet and
fragrant as befits their home." He speaks with
such yearning love of their common home—"This
kingdom limited alone by one old populous green
wall"—that his friends half believe he will not
be able to tear himself away from it; but he goes
on to speak of the success that shall be his, with a
look that breaks their dream. "That look," says
Festus, "as if where'er you gazed there stood a
star!" but yet "a solitary briar the bank puts forth
to save our swan's nest floating out to sea," and he
seeks to dissuade the boy from his scheme. Paracelsus protests that it was Festus himself who had
first awakened his mind, and guided him through
doubt and fear, though now trying to make him
reject God's great commission, his acceptance of
which is due to Festus's own teaching: "We agreed
as to what was man's end and God's will, and yet

[1] Martineau.

now that I am about to put it all into practice, you seem to hold that the sovereign proof that we devote ourselves to God, is seen in living just as though no God there were."

Festus, like many an elder since, accustomed to combine intellectual perception of truths with "respectable" inaction, is startled when enthusiastic youth thinks that acting upon a truth is the necessary consequence of perceiving it! But he goes on to recall Paracelsus's early life, and how he had come to stand apart from his compeers with a brooding purpose to gain—

> "The secret of the world,
> Of man, and man's true purpose, path, and fate,
> .   .   .   .   .
> You, if a man may, dare aspire to KNOW."

Paracelsus protests against his aim being stated thus, and declares that he aspires to nothing but to give a ready answer to the will of God, "who summons me to be His organ." Festus bids him search well into his heart, to see whether his ruling motive be not ambition rather than God's glory, warning him that God appoints no less the way of praise than the desire of praise—

> " Presume not to serve God apart from such
> Appointed channels as He wills shall gather
> Imperfect tributes—for that sole obedience
> Valued, perchance. He seeks not that His altars
> Blaze, careless how, so that they do but blaze."

Paracelsus replies that he requires "no fairer seal" to his mission than the fierce energy, the irresistible force, that work within him, since God—

" Ne'er dooms to waste the strength He deigns impart . .
  They sleep not whom God needs : "

through him "new hopes shall animate the world." Festus asks why he should strike out new paths, instead of following up the work of those who had been before him.   He answers that, from his youth, a secret influence has been about him to which he turned—

"Scarce consciously, as turns
A water-snake where fairies cross his sleep,"

and this spirit has ever been calling upon him to separate himself from mankind, and to do the world some mighty service, seeking for no rewards—

" Like some knight traversing a wilderness
  Who on his way may chance to free a tribe
  Of desert people from their dragon foe,
  When all the swarthy tribes press round to kiss
  His feet, and choose him for their king, and yield
  Their poor tents, pitched among the sand-hills, for
  His realm ; and he points, smiling, to his scarf,
  Heavy with riveted gold, his burgonet,
  Gay set with twinkling stones—and to the East,
  Where these must be displayed."

After a youth spent in feelings such as these, there came a period of conscious failure as he worked with the other students.   At last—when it dawned upon him that he seemed less successful than his fellows only because his aims were larger—a voice said to him, "Whence spring defeat and loss? Even from thy strength;" "and I smiled, as men never smile but once; then first discovering my own aim's extent, which sought to comprehend God and His works. From that time all things wore a different hue to me, and now I go to prove my soul! I see my way as birds their trackless way. In some good time I shall arrive. He guides me and the bird. In His good time!" Festus again urges upon him to accept the light of those who have gone before, but he refuses to sit beside their dry wells—

" While in the distance heaven is blue above
    Mountains where sleep the unsunned tarns."

Festus yields to his ardour, and Michal exclaims: "Then Aureole is God's commissary! He shall be great and grand!" " No, sweet," says he, "not great and grand; I never will be served by those I serve!"

With an insight justified by the end, Festus warns him against being " that monstrous spectacle upon the earth, a being knowing not what love is." Replying first to the old objection, Paracelsus denies that he is wrong in rejecting the wisdom gained by others, because truth is within ourselves, and to KNOW consists in opening out a way for this imprisoned splendour to escape; some seemingly commonplace man may go mad, and—

> " By his wild talk alone,
> You first collect how great a spirit he had."

Paracelsus says his aim is to discover the true laws by which " the flesh accloys the spirit." Is not this the aim that St. Paul proposes to us, when he exhorts us to " grow in the knowledge of the Son of God, unto *a perfect man*, unto the measure of the stature of the fulness of Christ " ?

> " Let us not always say,
> ' Spite of this flesh, to-day
> I strove, made head, gained ground upon the whole.'
> As the bird wings and sings,
> Let us cry, ' All good things
> Are ours, nor soul helps flesh more, now, than flesh helps
> soul.' "

Ascetics were wrong—they looked on the spirit as everything, and on the body as a mere opportunity of mortifying and disciplining that spirit; and still more wrong were those of the Renaissance, who thought only of beautifying and perfecting the body and the intellect. Paracelsus saw that man's true perfection must be in perfecting body *and* spirit—that the body ought to be a help, and not a hindrance, in leading the higher life. He sought to find the laws by the observance of which would best be furthered man's development as a perfect whole. How to do this seems to be still the main problem of the day, the yet unanswered riddle of the sphinx. How, indeed, could it be otherwise, since to solve it would be to understand life and God's education of the human race? But to return to the argument of Paracelsus: he says, with regard to the scorn of love and gratitude with which Festus taxes him, that when he has achieved his aim and KNOWS, his affections, laid to sleep awhile, will awaken purified.

> " Till then, till then . . .
> Ah, the time—whiling loitering of a page,
> Thro' bower and over lawn, till eve shall bring
> The stately lady's presence whom he loves ;
> The broken sleep of the fisher, whose rough coat
> Enwraps the queenly pearl—these are faint types."

Then, with one only touch of human weakness (feeling with Novalis, who said, " My belief gains infinitely the moment it is shared by one other human soul"), he breaks off with—" Say, do you believe I shall accomplish this?" " I do believe," says Festus. " I ever did," says Michal.

Nine years later, Paracelsus sits in the house of a Greek conjurer in Constantinople, while against the splendour of the setting sun, " the city, black and crooked, runs like a Turk verse along a scimitar." This fortune-teller wills that his seekers should inscribe their previous life's attainments in his roll, before his promised secret shall make up the sum. Accordingly (" slipped into the blank space between an idiot's gibber and a mad lover's ditty "), a few blurred characters record how Paracelsus had wandered through many lands, and made a few discoveries, though too intent on coming gain to stay and scrutinize the little gained. The Greek had promised that he should not quit the chamber till he should know what he desired; and as he sits waiting, he muses on his past life, and how he had bent it unceasingly to his one purpose; and then (for he ever " bears a memory of a pleasant life, whose small events he treasures ") his thoughts wander back to Einsiedeln, his earliest home, and to Festus, with " that sweet maiden long ago his bride," and then he recalls the early days of his search after truth, when all the wonder and beauty of life were as the mere robe of truth : he sees the robe now, he saw the form then. He had never paused upon his way, had never glanced behind to see if his primal light had waned; and thus insensibly he had declined from his high level. Then he prays— " Crush not my mind, dear God, tho' I be crushed ; give but one hour of my first energy, that I may mould the truths I have, and so completing them, possess."

He is interrupted by the lovely song (" I heard a voice, perchance I heard, long ago, but too low "), in which—

" All poets that God meant
Should save the world, and therefore lent
Great gifts to, but who, proud, refused
To do His work, or lightly used
Those gifts, or failed, thro' weak endeavour,
Now mourn, cast off by Him forever."

Then enters the sweet singer, Aprile, who proclaims that the ambition of his life had been " to love infinitely and be loved ; " and as he tells of the world of love and loveliness which he had aspired to create, and how he had been distracted from his mission by the very sense of beauty which had been intrusted to him in order that he might fulfil it,—Paracelsus, in the darkness, softens into tears, exclaiming, " Merciful God ! forgive us both. I too have sought to KNOW, as thou to LOVE, excluding love as thou refusedst knowledge." But even as he implores Aprile to live with him till both are saved (they being " two halves of one dissevered world whom this strange chance unites "), Aprile dies upon his breast, surrounded by visions of " white brows, lit up with glory, poets all," exclaiming, " God is the perfect poet, who in His own person acts His own creations." " Let me love," says Paracelsus ; " I have attained, and now I may depart."

Five years later, Paracelsus, the wondrous life-dispenser, Fate's commissary, idol of the schools and courts, sits in his own chamber at Basle, heaping on " logs to let the blaze laugh out," as

K

he listens to Festus's account of the quiet life
which has been going on at Einsiedeln during his
own wild wanderings, and of Michal, whose face
"still wears that quiet and peculiar light, like the
dim circlet floating round a pearl," although her
children are "wild with joy beside her;" but
Paracelsus cares not to hear of them, for they
unsettle the old picture in his mind.

> "Michal may become her motherhood,
> But 'tis a change, and I detest all change,
> And most, a change in aught I loved long since."

And so the talk goes on, till Festus humbly says —

> "But you are very kind to humour me
> By showing interest in my quiet life."

And Paracelsus answers that Death lets out
strange secrets; that some few weeks ago he had
helped a man to die—a courtier, who had "well-
nigh wormed all traces of God's finger out of him,"
and yet an hour before his death—

> "Having laid long with blank and soulless eyes,
> He sat up suddenly, and with natural voice,
> Said that, in spite of thick air and closed doors,
> God told him it was June; and he knew well,
> Without such telling, hare-bells grew in June;
> And all that kings could ever give or take
> Would not be precious as those blooms to him.
> Just so . . . it seems to me much worthier argument,

Why pansies, eyes that laugh, bear beauty's prize
From violets, eyes that dream (your Michal's choice),
Than all fools find to wonder at in me
Or in my fortunes ! "

And then he breaks out into sneers at his own
popularity in the schools, accusing himself of
quackery, confessing the utter failure of his aspira-
tions, and his inner misery only hidden by his fame
and seeming success. Festus, amazed, refuses to
believe him, recounts the wonders told by all of
his healing power, how he was—

" One ordained
To free the flesh from fell disease, as frees
Our Luther's burning tongue the fettered soul."

Paracelsus persists in declaring that he has thrown
his life away, and that, bought by a hollow popularity, based on ignorance, he has subsided into
enjoying a lower range of pleasures than of old.
He tells how Aprile had warned him that the only
way to save himself was to serve his fellows ; and
how he had therefore come to be teacher and
physician in Basle, where crowds were crying
" Hosanna !" to-day, who would be just as eager in
crying " Crucify !" to-morrow. He had found it
impossible to live for love and beauty like Aprile
—the old craving for knowledge had come upon
him again, though now he lived on a lower level,
and was haunted by the fear that he might sink
still more, and come to breathe falsehood as if it

were truth. Festus assures him this mood will
pass.

> " Be brave, dear Aureole, since
> The rabbit has his shade to frighten him,
> The fawn a rustling bough, mortals their cares,
> And higher natures yet would slight and laugh
> At these entangling fantasies, as you
> At trammels of a weaker intellect.
> Measure your mind's height by the shade it casts."

He rejects Paracelsus's suggestion that he is blinded
by his love.

> " Nought blinds you less than admiration, friend !
> Whether it be that all love renders wise
> In its degree : from love which blends with love—
> Heart answering heart—to love which spends itself
> In silent, mad idolatry of some
> Pre-eminent mortal, some great soul of souls,
> Which ne'er will know how well it is adored :
> I say, such love is never blind ; but rather
> Alive to every, the minutest spot
> Which mars its object, and which hate (supposed
> So vigilant and searching) dreams not of :
> Love broods on such—What then ? When first perceived
> Is there no sweet strife to forget, to change,
> To overflush these blemishes with all
> The glow of general goodness they disturb ?
> To make these very defects an endless source
> Of new affections grown from hopes and fears ? "

Paracelsus exclaims at his being thus instructed
by a quiet mountain-cloistered priest, but goes on
to point out where his sole merit lies : namely, in
being in advance of his age, though he fears his

clumsy pupils will fail to use aright the intellectual weapons with which he has furnished them. Then the melancholy wind disturbs the talk, and Festus, opening the casement, looks out into the night, where "peaceful sleep the tree-tops all together!" "Like an asp the wind slips whispering from bough to bough, 'Morn is near'"—

> " The shrubs bestir and rouse themselves as if
> Some snake that weighed them down all night, let go
> His hold, and from the east, fuller and fuller,
> Day, like a mighty river, is flowing in,
> But clouded, wintry, desolate, and cold "—

a dawn in keeping with the wounded heart, which cries out that knowledge belongs to God and His spirits, while—

> " Love, hope, fear, faith—these make humanity,
> These are its signs, its note, its character,
> And these I've lost !—gone, shut from me forever,
> Like a dead friend, safe from unkindness more ! "

The friends next meet, two years later, at an inn in Alsatia. Paracelsus is on his way to Nuremberg because of his unpopularity in Basle, where he has received "hate, scorn, obloquy, and all the higher, rarer, and more gratifying forms of popular applause."[1] As long as he merely satisfied their love of the marvellous, they worshipped him; but when he strove to teach them real truth, he reaped truth's usual reward—a crown of thorns.

---

[1] Prof. Seeley.

He announces his intention of seeking anew his former goal, but by better means than the old ones, over which he sings the lovely dirge, " Heap cassia, sandal buds;" he will accept all help, he says, instead of spurning it as before—he will not only *know*, but will also *enjoy* every delight that comes in his path, and his future shall be glorious with visions of a full success. But Festus is not blinded by this feverish eagerness, and Paracelsus says he is glad of it—glad that Festus is not "gulled by all this swaggering," but can see how full he is of mean motives and low desires. In vain does Festus strive to assure him that these feelings are no part of his real nature ; he refuses comfort, and declares he has nothing left but that " this life of mine must be lived out and a grave thoroughly earned." Festus urges him to make a mighty effort to redeem the past, and even yet to arrive at his destination; but he declares it is too late, and sings the tale of those who sailed in a gallant armament, bearing on each ship a fair statue, for which they were to build shrines on certain islands. Weary of their voyage, they landed on the first rock they came to—

> " All day we built its shrine for each, . . .
> Nor paused, till, in the westering sun,
> We sat together on the beach
> To sing because our work was done."

As they rested, came a raft with gentle islanders.

" 'Our isles are just at hand,' they cried, . . .
'Our olive groves thick shades are keeping
For these majestic forms,' they cried ;
Oh, when we woke with sudden start
From our deep dream, and knew too late
How bare the rock, how desolate,
Which had received our precious freight ;
Yet, we called out, ' Depart !
Our gifts, once given, must here abide.
We have no heart to mar our work !' we cried."

And so, with Paracelsus, he now knew the barren-
ness of the rock whereon he had built; but he had
no heart to rear a fresh shrine for his soul; his
nature was no longer even pure enough to return,
as Festus wished, to his quiet home at Einsiedeln.
His life was broken, his trust in God had proved a
broken reed. But here Festus interrupted him,
declaring what he had called "trust" was nothing
but self-delusion and selfishness.

"None
Could trace God's will so plain as you, while yours
Remained implied in it. But now you fail,
And we, who prate about that will, are fools !"

Paracelsus retorts that Man is the glory of God,
and that he had promoted God's glory in striving
to be glorious himself. He says again, that the old
life is not for him ; that he must dree his weird,
however Festus may scorn him; that he departs
secure against all further insult; " my one friend's
scorn shall brand me ; no fear of sinking deeper !

Only never let Michal know this last dull winding up of all; grieve her not." "Your ill-success can little grieve her now;" whereat Paracelsus, in an ecstasy of sorrow, knowing well that, with her, indifference to his fate means death, assures Festus, as if it were some strange discovery of his own, that she yet lives in spirit.

> " Know, then, you did not ill to trust your love
> To the cold earth: I have thought much of it,
> For I believe we do not wholly die.

And so we leave him musing on how Michal sleeps amidst the roots and dews, and on what an empty farce are his schemes and struggles, compared to the reality of the loss he has just learned.

Thirteen years later, Festus sits by his friend's death-bed, in the hospital of Sebastian, at Salzburg, listening in unavailing sorrow to his delirium, crying vainly to God for him : "Save him, dear God ! Thou art not made like us ; we should be wroth in such a case, but Thou forgivest !" But the sick man ceases not to rave and to rail at the fiends who have marred his work, and who are now triumphing over his failure. He wails over his loss of both power and love.

> " Sweet human love is gone !
> 'Tis only when they spring to heaven that angels
> Reveal themselves to you : they sit all day

Beside you, and lie down at night by you
Who care not for their presence—muse or sleep—
And all at once, they leave you, and you know them.
We are so fooled, so cheated ! "

At last he awakens to his friend's presence, and fancies himself once more at Einsiedeln, watching St. Saviour's spire flame in the sunset—

"All its figures quaint
Gay in the glancing light. You might conceive them
A troop of yellow-vested, white-haired Jews,
Bound for their own land, where redemption dawns."

And then he yields the fight, accuses himself of quackery and deceit, and prays to be "forgotten even by God." Festus refuses to believe his failure and bids him enter gloriously his rest.

"'I am for noble Aureole, God !' cries he.
'I am upon his side, come weal or woe.
His portion shall be mine : he has done well.
I would have sinned, had I been strong enough,
As he has sinned ; reward him or I waive
Reward ! If Thou canst find no place for him,
He shall be king elsewhere, and I will be
His slave forever. There are two of us.'"

"Speak on," says Paracelsus, "or I dream ; " and Festus soothes him with the song—

"There the Mayne glideth,
Where my love abideth,"

till its simple words loose the sick man's heart, and

drive out the darkness which naught else could touch.

> " Like some dark snake that force may not expel,
>   He glideth out to music sweet and low."

And then his mind awakens wholly, and he arises, with a last effort of strength, to tell God's message. He bids Festus not deem his aims wrong, for he goes joyous back to God, although he brings no offering. " Higher prizes may await the mortal persevering to the end;" but yet he is not all so valueless, though he too soon left following the instincts of that happy time when he had vowed himself to man. He was born with all the high ambitions of which others only attain the perception by many struggles and mistakes; he had felt and known what God was and how He dwelt in the whole of life, most of all, in man, in whom were united, in a wondrous whole, the dim fragments of glory found in the rest of creation. In man, Paracelsus now saw, "*Power* neither blind nor all knowing, but checked by hope and fear; *knowledge*, not intuition, as he had once thought, but the slow fruit of toil; *love*, not serenely pure, but strong through weakness —a blind, oft-failing, yet believing love—a half enlightened, often chequered trust." And in man thus formed, all nature receives a soul. When he once appears in the world—

> " The winds are henceforth voices, in a wail or shout,
> A querulous mutter, or a quick, gay laugh ;
> Never a senseless gust now man is born."

Yet all this is only to teach us man's proper place, to which he has not yet attained, and never will, till " all mankind alike is perfected, equal in full-blown powers ;" when this is consummated, then will " his long triumphant march begin." Even as, before man's advent, all that was highest in Nature was but a symbol and foreshadowing of him, so, when he is perfected, shall he feel in himself—

> " August anticipations, symbols, types
> Of a dim splendour ever on before
> In that eternal circle life pursues."

His enlarged horizon shall fill him with new hopes and fears, unmeasured thirst for good.

> " Such men are even now upon the earth,
> Serene among the half-formed creatures round
> Who should be saved by them, and joined with them.
> Such was my task, and I was born for it.

" I from the first was never cheated by a delusive and divided aim, as has been the fate of many a high-dowered spirit ! I clearly saw that God was glorified in man, and to man's glory vowed I soul and limb. I never fashioned out a fancied good distinct from man's, and never dreamed that his successes could be over-great. Yet, clear-sighted,

gifted, still I failed. I thought *power* the sign
and note and character of man, and saw no reason
why he should not rise to it by one bold leap. I
sought for power alone, and that without the
discipline of tears and labour by which man, in the
future, shall attain to it—for he shall painfully attain
to joy, while love and hope shall keep him man—
and as my dreams grew dim, my wide aims
circumscribed by petty obstacles, what wonder if I
saw no way to shun despair? The power I sought
for man, seemed God's; then, from Aprile I
learned my error, and saw how one sin had spotted
my career from its uprise.

> " Love's undoing
> Taught me the worth of love in man's estate,
> And what proportion love should hold with power
> In his right constitution ; love preceding
> Power, and with much power, always much more love.

" I thought then that the whole was learned ; I
devoted all my knowledge to man's service, but
scorned their stupid wonder, despised their praise,
and when they turned upon me, it was not strange
I hated them, for—

> " In my own heart love had not been made wise
> To trace love's first beginnings in mankind.

" It is fitting that men should, at this present,
only see the weak and false in me, but in after-
times they yet shall know me.

"If I stoop
Into a dark, tremendous sea of cloud
It is but for a time. I press God's lamp
Close to my breast ; its splendour soon or late
Will pierce the gloom : I shall emerge one day."

And so, with brave words upon his lips, and clasping the hand of his earliest friend, the great sin-stained, storm-tossed spirit passes to that "world of larger scope," where "what here is faithfully begun will be completed, not undone."

"He there does now enjoy eternall rest,
Sleep after toyle, port after stormie seas,
Ease after warre, death after life does greatly please."

With the questioning spirit abroad on all sides, meeting one in every magazine, when it is a moot point whether life be worth living, it is a grand thing to be able to say, with Clough, to all the doubts which seek to paralyze our souls, "I know not ; I will do my duty." But it is grander still to hold, with Browning, that there *is* an answer to the thoughts which trouble us, another side to the pain, and grief, and failure, and littleness which crush us as we look upon life, and that we are justified in saying with Paracelsus, "One day I shall emerge." Beside the nettle grows the dock, and in this age of unbelief, which would fain believe, we have a prophet sent us, who brings a word of the Lord, translated into the thoughts and feelings of our own day, though it is, in truth, an old message, which many prophets and kings have desired to see, and could only see dimly afar off; a message which has strengthened the hearts of heroes in all ages, and inspired all " the communion of saints whose heroic sufferings rise up melodiously together to heaven, out of all lands, out of all times, as a sacred *Miserere ;* their heroic actions also as a boundless, everlasting psalm of triumph." [1]

Browning's " Men and Women " learn this truth, this faith in immortality, in many ways, even as the Easterns say in their proverb, " Jesus went many ways unto Jerusalem." Pompilia seizes it through her feeling of the necessity of another world, wherein can be manifested that wealth of undying love which finds no utterance here.

> " O, lover of my life, O, soldier-saint !
> No work begun shall ever pause for death.
> Love will be helpful to me more and more
> I' the coming course."

It is taught to Rabbi Ben Ezra by the very imperfection of man's nature.

> " Life shall succeed in that it seems to fail.
>> What I aspired to be
>> And was not, comforts me,
> A brute I might have been, but would not sink i' the scale."

>> " All I could never be
>> All men ignored in me ;
> This I was worth to God, whose wheel the pitcher shaped."

[1] " Sartor Resartus."

This life is but machinery just meant to give the soul its bent, to shape the pitcher ; the uses of the cup, the *raison d'être* of the soul, wait for the fuller life beyond, where will be the festal board—

> " The new wine's foaming flow,
> The Master's lips aglow."

It is his failure here which teaches Paracelsus the true greatness of his mission. Over and over again does Browning impress upon us that man's imperfections only show his real superiority.

> " What's whole can increase no more,
> Is dwarfed and dies, since here's its sphere."

In " Old Pictures at Florence," he argues that Christian artists are inferior to Greek, just because they strive to express a deeper meaning. Greek perfection of form was a sign of limitation, of inferiority in depth. Christian artists were more faulty, precisely because of their wider nature.

> " For time, theirs—ours for eternity.
> They are perfect—how else ? They shall never change.
> We are faulty—why not ? We have time in store."

The feeling, that we have time in store, is the keynote of the chord that closes " Paracelsus." He was one who learned to—

> " Throw on God
> (He loves the burthen)
> God's task to make the heavenly period
> Perfect the earthen."

What faith but this could support us in a world where many a noble heart sinks under failure and defeat, like him who breathed away his soul in the cry: "I have loved righteousness and hated iniquity, and therefore I die in exile"?

But Browning says, as the angel did to Esdras, "Lovest thou this people more than He that made them?"

> "Do I find Love so full in my nature, God's ultimate gift,
>   That I doubt His own love can compete with it, here the
>   parts shift?
>   Would I fain, in my impotent yearning, do all for this man,
>   And dare doubt He alone shall not help him, who yet
>   alone can?"

And like Paracelsus, Browning's own—

> "Heart *has* been made wise by love,
> To trace love's faint beginnings in mankind,
> To see a good in evil, and a hope
> In ill-success; to sympathize, be proud
> Of their half-reasons, faint aspirings, dim
> Struggles for truth, their poorest fallacies,
> Their prejudice, and fears and cares and doubts,
> All with a touch of nobleness, despite
> Their error, upward tending all, tho' weak,
> Like plants in mines which never saw the sun,
> But dream of him, and guess where he may be,
> And do their best to climb and get at him."

He faces man's littleness because he believes in his greatness. He can bear to confront the unsuccess of life, "contrast the petty done, the undone vast," for, in that very unsuccess, he sees a fairer promise for the end than if man were allowed in this world, "to plant his foot upon the goal— twine glory-garlands round his soul." Browning raises our conception of the race, not so much by dwelling on those who, like Paracelsus, stand out above their fellows spiritually, as Saul did physically, "from the shoulders upward higher than any of the people :" he rather dwells on " Saul the mistake, Saul the failure," and on that infinite love which shall—

> " Bid him awake
> From the dream, the probation, the prelude, to find him-
> self set,
> Clear and safe, in new light and new life—a new harmony,
> yet
> To be run and continued and ended.   Who knows ? "

"READ the canonical books of Literature, and let the smaller books take care of themselves," says Coleridge, and where shall we find any book more universally accepted as canonical than "The Divine Comedy"? But before we can read it, we must be acquainted with Dante's life, for his personal feelings form the thread which binds it together. When we look at Shakespeare we are inclined to feel that it needed his superhuman impersonality to make him not "of an age, but for all time," that, had he "unlocked his heart,"[1] he would have lost somewhat of his power over our hearts. It is surely a true feeling that egotism means smallness and makes poets as well as other people forgotten. But, with Dante, egotism meant greatness, and has made all the world know and remember him. It may be questioned whether, since the world began, there has ever been a man with such a strong personality as his : it runs through every line of his poem, and to enter into that poem we must realize the two main strands in his thread of life,—love for Beatrice, and love for Florence. The man who

[1] Matthew Arnold.

so intensely loved the two fairest things the world
then held, was bound to have a " Fair Soul," and
he shows it to us in the "Vita Nuova," the most
beautiful love story ever written, in which he tells
us of his love for Beatrice Portinari. Who has not
pictured the first meeting of those two Florentine
children, at the great feast given by Folco Portinari,
to celebrate the coming of May? not the "pious
fraud of the almanacs,"[1] which we know under that
name, but the Italian May, the spring-time of the
Poets. We see the boy, as Boccaccio describes
him, serving at the tables, and then playing with
the children, among whom was the little lady of
the house, in that dress which so dwelt in her boy-
lover's fancy, "of a most noble colour, a subdued
crimson," and with those "grave and consecrated
eyes,"[2] whose light was to be his guiding star
through this world and the next. "Often in my
boyish years," he tells us, "did I go in search of
this youngest of the angels, and sometimes, as she
passed along the street, she turned her eyes to
where I stood, thrilled through and through, and,
by her ineffable courtesy, which now hath its
guerdon in everlasting life, she saluted me in such
gracious wise, that I seemed to see heaven in all
its blessedness."

But, though he must have daily seen her who
was "so near and yet so far," they seldom spoke,

[1] J. R. Lowell.   [2] Ben Jonson.

for he records each greeting with religious care—
" the hour her most sweet salutation reached me
was the ninth hour of the day." He was happy in
this distant awestruck worship, and his friends
listened to his sonnets on his " gentil donna," with
an understanding patience, which makes us wonder
whether that age of blood and iron was not, in
some ways, gentler than our own. Sounds of
kindly laughter come to us here and there, from
these fortressed houses of Dante's Florence,—as
from that company of ladies who, one day, ask
him, " Wherein, we pray thee, abides that happiness
of thine ? " The poet finds the kindliness beneath
the laughter, and gives an answer in language that
breathes the whole spirit of chivalry, " In the
words which praise my lady."

In 1286, his lady married Simon dei Bardi, the
spiritual ancestor of Romola, but this was no bar
to such reverential worship as Dante's. He went
on pouring out his soul in the poems with which
the prose story of the " Vita Nuova " is interspersed,
the loveliest being that which begins : " Ladies
who have intelligence of Love," in which he tells
how the angels besought God that they might have
Beatrice to be with them in Paradise, and how He
refused, " for the sake of one on earth who loves
her, and who dreads to lose her."

But his dread was soon to overshadow him : four
years later he breaks off in the middle of a sonnet

with the verse from the Vulgate : " How doth the city sit solitary that was full of people." The city of Florence was now solitary to him, for Beatrice was dead. This is the end of Dante's earthly love story; the end, as it seemed to him, of that Vita Nuova, that new life, which was born in him through knowing Beatrice, but it was the beginning of his real life. He was scarcely a man as yet, only twenty-five, but this feeling of his boyhood was to be the mainspring of his future life, the inspiration of that marvellous life-work at which he hints in the concluding words of the " Vita Nuova," where he strikes a chord that is worthy to close the requiem of such a loss.

" I resolved to speak no more of this blessed one, until the time should come when I could speak of her more worthily. And to arrive at this, I study as much as I can, as she truly knows : so that, if it pleaseth Him, by whom all things live, that my life should continue for a time, I hope to say that of her which has not yet been spoken of any woman. And after, may it please Him, who is the Lord of Courtesy, that my soul may see the glory of my Lady, that blessed Beatrice, who gloriously beholds the Face of Him who is blessed for ever."

But he was not yet fit to write of her worthily. " No one shall sing a song to the Immortals," says one of our own singers,[1]" who cannot live the song

---

[1] G. MacDonald.

he sings, for what right hath he else to take holy deeds in his mouth;" and Milton also tells us, that "he who would write a true poem must first make his life a true poem." Dante had "the poet's heart and brain, feeling and song," but he himself was not yet "a poem of God's making."[1] Beautiful feelings alone never make a hero, the fire of the forge will never make a sword without the smith's hammer; and Dante needed to be forged and hammered by the blows of real life and duty and hard work for his country.

Let us put him in his place in history before we go on to the more historical part of his life. He was born in 1265, when our Henry III., the "monarch of the simple life," was reigning; he died in 1321, during the troubles of our Edward II. When he was a boy the Crusades had just come to an end. St. Louis died 1270. Cimabue was becoming the father of Italian painting, and training Giotto, who was afterwards to learn even higher inspiration from his friendship with Dante.

While Dante was worshipping Beatrice, Edward I. was conquering Wales; while he was a man of business in Florence, Edward was crushing William Wallace; and while he was in exile, writing his poem, Robert Bruce was beginning to free Scotland. We shall meet with our Henry III. in Purgatory, one of the few Englishmen to whom

[1] G. MacDonald, "Within and Without."

Dante gives a place in his Temple of Fame; but one cannot help feeling that when the poet did, in very deed, and not in vision, join the company of the Blessed, he would have had more sympathy with Edward I., who was akin to his own strong and disdainful soul.

In the second stage of Dante's life, to which we now come, Florence is his first thought; hitherto she has only been a background for Beatrice,—now he plunges into active life, and learns to love his city only second to his lady. In 1293, when he wrote those closing words of the " Vita Nuova," he was one of the priors, or chief rulers, of Florence; a stern, sad man, in a city torn asunder by the strifes of Guelphs, and Ghibellines, Bianchi and Neri. After seven years of faithful service in the ranks of the Guelphs, the Papal party, he was sent, in 1300, on an embassy to Rome.

In the following year the Ghibelline or Imperialist party gained the upper hand, and passed sentence of banishment on their opponents, including the absent Dante. He never returned to his home, though for twenty years he thundered night and day at the gates of Florence, while he learnt "how salt was the bread of others, and how steep their stairs." Yet he would not return unworthily, and when the magistrates of Florence offered a safe return to such exiles as would do penance for their offences, he sent them an answer which rings still with the fiery scorn of that most "disdainful soul":—"Is this the glorious revocation of an unjust sentence, by which Dante Alighieri is to be recalled, after suffering almost three lustres of exile? Is this the recompense of labour? May such cowardice and earthly baseness of heart be far from me. Another way might surely be found which would not derogate from the honour of Dante. Such would I accept, and not with slow steps. But if with this way only I can return to Florence, Florence shall never again be entered by me. And what then? Can I not still behold the sun and stars? Cannot I still ponder upon truth under the free heavens?"

Yet he would have moved heaven and earth for that boon which he refused to take ignobly,—he wandered all over Europe (some say even to Oxford), with but this one thought in his mind, so far as earthly things were concerned. Spiritually, his wanderings led him to Hell and Heaven, so that women in the street would point him out to their children, saying, "Look! that man has been to Hell, and that is why his hair is so scorched and grizzled." And truly, Dante's intense realization of the unseen could not fail to leave traces on him. We say now that a description is "Dantesque," when it makes us actually see something grim and terrible;—no wonder that, as he says himself, his poem made him "lean." We read his bitter disappointment in every page,—it shows us a man hard and stern, yet with flashes, every now and then, of an infinite tenderness and compassion, which bring back to us the boy who had been such a true lover of Beatrice. We cannot wonder at the hardness in a man who lost all personal joy in life when he was twenty-five, who worked day and night for his country for ten years, and, as a reward, was turned adrift to wander in heart-broken exile for twenty years, smarting with the intense feeling of injustice from the city he had loved so well.

His life was a failure to the last; his lady married another, and died young; his city was ungrateful; he never had any honour that he cared for. Bologna offered him a crown of laurels; but he cared for no crown that was not Florentine. "Were it not better," he says, "to veil these grey hairs, that once were golden, beside my native Arno, with the crown that is given there?"

But he never saw his native Arno again, though it was never out of sight of his mind's eye: he peoples the slopes of Hell and Purgatory and Heaven with Florentines, never letting us forget the Lady of Cities, any more than we forget Beatrice.

But his failure to gain Florence has gained him the whole world. He might never rest again on the Sasso di Dante, that stone still standing in the great square of Florence, where tradition tells us Dante used to sit and watch Arnulpho building his cathedral; but he has achieved the Siege Perilous, among the noble army of poets, who must perforce be a " noble army of martyrs," and " learn in suffering what they teach in song."

The Divine Comedy.

M R. LOWELL speaks somewhere of "literature suited to desolate islands." To use
his idea in a somewhat different sense than his
context allows, I will ask what book you would
advise Robinson Crusoe to save from the wreck,
if only one were allowed him?

In my own case, supposing I looked forward to
an eventual return to civilized life, I would take
Shakespeare as being the most humanizing of
writers, the most likely to sustain, in a shipwrecked
man, the urbane, serene temper which he would
need in future intercourse with his fellows. But
were the banishment to be perpetual, I would take
Dante, as the writer who most keenly recognizes
the human interests of life, and yet keeps steadily
in view the supreme end of tuning our nature for
a higher life.

As it is an education in itself to go to pictures
with an artist—to music with a musician,—so it is
an education to go to Life with Dante, one who
can teach us to " see life steadily and see it whole." [1]

The " Commedia " is a book of practical spiritual

[1] Matthew Arnold.

counsel, for Dante here gives us a faithful transcript
of his own inner life.   The " Purgatorio " especially
is one of the great autobiographies of the world, as
much so as the " Confessions of St. Augustine."
When we read these confessions of Dante we see
his nature developing under the discipline of life.
It surely cannot be merely a sense of dramatic
fitness that causes each division of the poem to
exhibit him in a new stage of growth.

Years of experience (though, maybe, not of
months) must have been lived through, before the
Dante of the " Inferno," the disdainful man of the
world, was transformed into the humble pilgrim of
the " Purgatorio," or attained to the burning purity
of the pupil of Beatrice in the " Paradiso."   The
transitions follow the order one would, from his circumstances, naturally expect.   In the early days of
exile, he was likely to be hotly indignant, eager to
see the Day of Vengeance ; but as time passed on,
he would be " made great " by the " loving correc-
tion " of his life ; he would realize his own shortcomings, and be more generous to those of others.
The Dante who felt, in the " Inferno," about Fra
Alberigo, " that to be rude to him was courtesy,"
speaks of the meanest sinners in the " Purgatorio " as
" those beloved souls."   It is this personal element
that makes the poem so fascinating even in a translation.   Many wait till they can read Italian
forgetting that the original will have double charm

if they are familiar beforehand with the matter of
the poem, and that with such translations as
Longfellow, Plumptre, and Vernon, they can even
now enjoy the careful character study with which
Dante draws Virgil and Beatrice ; and the sketches
of such men as Farinata, " who had hell in great
despite," or of Jason, " the tall one who retained
his royal aspect and for his pain seemed not to
shed a tear ; " they will enjoy Dante's close study of
Nature, specially of bird life ;—and his many lines
which embody some helpful, devotional thought (a
whole manual of Intercessory Prayer might be com-
plied from the " Purgatorio)." Read the " Commedia " and mark it, make a subject concordance
for yourselves, note down marginal references com-
paring one passage with another, and you will come
to feel that Dante fills all earth and Heaven with
new light, and has an echo for every beautiful sight
you see, every noble word you hear.

His geography needs a word of explanation : the
belief of his day was that Lucifer fell from Heaven
on to the Garden of Eden, and by the impetus of
his fall pushed the garden right through the earth.
Lucifer himself stuck fast at the centre of the globe,
but the earth which he had dislodged rose out of
the Southern Ocean as the Mount of Purgatory,
bearing on its summit the Garden of Eden, or the
Terrestrial Paradise. The opening made in the
northern hemisphere by Lucifer's fall, was covered

over by a crust of earth, on which was built Jerusalem, while the crater-like hollow beneath was peopled by lost souls, the sins of Passion, Heresy, and Malevolence, being punished in separate circles of the ever-narrowing descent. Dante, led by Virgil, descends this funnel-shaped Inferno, and after he passes Lucifer (who is at the centre of gravity), a narrow passage leads him through the Earth to the Mount of Purgatory.

There are seven terraces on this mountain, with a staircase leading from one to the other, and, on each terrace, Dante finds a special sin being punished. When any soul is cleansed from that sin, it mounts up to the next terrace ; till at last it works its way through all seven circles, and, purged from the seven Deadly Sins, rises to the Earthly Paradise, the foretaste of the joys of Heaven. After ascending the mountain, Dante is translated by Beatrice to each of the nine heavens which, like so many coats of an onion, encompass the earth. Each of these heavens is the home of souls distinguished by some special virtue, and all are enclosed by the Empyrean, the motionless sphere of Light, the Home of God Himself, where all the saints have their appointed station, and help to form the mystic Rose, whose petals are the Blessed Company of all faithful people.

With this general sketch by which to find our bearings, let us follow Dante a little more closely in his pilgrimage. When the poem opens he is midway on the road of life, and finds himself " within a forest dark," as one " who weeps in all his thoughts and is despondent." He meets one " from long continued silence hoarse," who urged him to " climb the Mount Delectable, which is the source and cause of every joy," where they dwell—

> " Who contented are
> Within the fire, because they hope to come
> Whene'er it may be, to the blessed people."

This is Virgil, who tells him that for his sake " Beatrice withdrew from singing Hallelujah," and came to the outer court of Hell, to invoke Virgil's aid for "a friend of hers, but not the friend of fortune." Virgil, exhorting Dante to take heart, seeing that " such ladies benedight are caring for him in the Courts of Heaven," leads him through the Gate of Hell with its inscription—

> " All hope abandon, ye who enter here."

There—

> " Voices high and hoarse
> Resounded through the air without a star."

Here were the melancholy souls of those " with neither infamy nor praise," " miscreants, who never were alive," such men as he " who made through cowardice the great refusal." Virgil speaks

after Dante's own heart when he says disdainfully,
"Let us not talk of them, but look and pass."
They are then ferried across Acheron by Charon,
and enter Limbo, the first Circle of Hell, where
there—

> "Were lamentations none, but only sighs
> That tremulous made the everlasting air."

Here dwelt the noble heathen, "only so far
punished," says Virgil, "that without hope we
live on in desire." Four mighty shades approach
to welcome Virgil on his return; "semblance had
they nor sorrowful nor glad," but Virgil smiled for
joy at their welcome of Dante when they adopted
him "sixth, mid so much wit." With these sages,
Dante passed on to the Castle of Human Wisdom,
defended by a fair rivulet and seven lofty walls.
Here in a meadow of fresh verdure were people
with—

> "Solemn eyes and slow,
> Of great authority in their countenance,"

"who spake but seldom and with gentle voices,"
mighty spirits, "whom to have seen," says Dante,
"I felt myself exalted." Among them are "Cæsar
in armour, with gerfalcon eyes;" "sitting alone,
apart, the Saladin;" and Aristotle, "the master of
those who know."

Dante passes from this noble company to a
place, "mute of all light," where the souls are

hurtled onwards by a hurricane, "as the wings of starlings bear them on," and as the cranes—

> "Go chanting forth their lays,
>   Making in air a long line of themselves."

These are the souls who sinned through Love, Helen, Paris, Tristram, and two who clung together as we see them in the pictures of Watts and Ary Scheffer, and who at Dante's call flew to him as—

> "Turtle doves called onward by desire,
>   With open and steady wings to the sweet nest."

They are Paolo and Francesa da Rimini, to whom "a sorrow's crown of sorrow is remembering happier things." One of the few touches of graciousness in the "Inferno" is the picture of these two, saying to Dante—

> "If were the King of the Universe our friend,
>   We would pray unto Him to give thee peace."

Dante swoons for sorrow at their story, and awakes to find himself in the third circle, where the gluttons are punished by rain, "eternal, maledict, and cold and heavy." Then come the avaricious—

> "Whose undiscerning life which made them sordid,
>   Now makes them unto all discernment dim."

In the fifth circle, the wrathful are tearing each

M

other in the sombre waters of Styx, while, further
on, are those who sinned through Accidie, the
spiritual sloth, which we rechristen "depression"
and "low spirits," and meet with sympathy!
Dante met it by fixing its victims in the mire
beneath the water, where they keep gurgling in
their throats the confession—

> "We sullen were
> In the sweet air, which by the sun is gladdened,
> Bearing within ourselves the sluggish reek ;
> Now we are sullen in this sable mire."

But we must not linger over each step of the
journey. The descent into Hell leads us through
"malign grey shores" and "filthy fens;" the air,
full of smoke and gloom, is thick with "accents
of anger, words of agony." Dante, with his Italian
love of light and warmth, "shivers in the eternal
shade," beholding—

> "A thousand faces, made
> Purple with cold ; whence o'er me comes a shudder,
> And evermore will come, at frozen ponds."

The City of Dis stands out amid the gloom, with
its vermilion minarets and mosques, reflected in
the waves of the marshy lagoon that surrounds it.
Its gates are closed to the pilgrims till the celestial
messenger comes, heralded by the clangour as of
"a wind that smites the forest and, laden with

dust, onward goes superb." The ruined souls flee before him, as frogs before the hostile serpent, while he passes " o'er the Styx with soles unwet," silent and motionless save that he fans the heavy air from off his face, admired by Dante for the disdain with which he spake no word to them—

> " But had the look
> Of one whom other care constrains and goads
> Than that of him who in his presence is."

But when the gates fly open at his command, the city and its threatening citizens have vanished, as in a dream, and Dante finds himself wandering through a place of tombs, where lie the Heretics. Hitherto we have seen sins of Passion allied to those for which the pains of Purgatory have cleansing power, but Heresy was the sin of choosing evil instead of good, a denial of the higher principle of life which could alone raise man above his animal nature. Hence the City of Dis, with the Heretics in burning tombs, is the next halting-place before Malebolge, where we find the blacker sins of malevolence, beginning in violence, and ending in treachery and revolt against authority.

Three scenes stand out in the more accursed region to which we have now descended.

First, the sand waste, where—

> " Were raining down dilated flakes of fire,
> As of the snow on Alps without a wind."

We see the "dance of miserable hands, shaking from off them" these flakes of fire, and we see, too, the mighty one, "who heeded not the fire, but lay disdainful there, so that the rain seemed not to ripen him."

Next, Malebolge, a lake of pitch divided into circular rivers by concentric rings of stone causeways, on which the pilgrims walked, following the ring till they came to the bridge which led to the next and smaller causeway. Here they watch, with terrified sympathy, the tormented souls driven under the boiling pitch by demons with tridents, as busy at their task as Venetian workmen caulking their vessels at the Arsenal.

In the centre of this stone spider's-web, woven on the pitch lake, is the steep descent to the frozen Lake of Cocytus, where Lucifer for ever devours the traitors against God and the Empire.

Read Mr. Bryce's "Holy Roman Empire" to see why Dante puts the betrayal of Christ and of Cæsar on an equal footing. Much of Dante's strongest feeling is lost on us, unless we realize that to him the Empire was as Divine as the Papacy, and that each in its own sphere represented God's Authority. Herein lies the force of that denunciation of Constantine's marriage dower, which so pleased Virgil that he caught Dante in his arms and bore him—

> "Tenderly on the crag uneven and steep,
> That would have been hard passage for the goats."

In this thought lies the sting of Sordello's disappointment in " German Albert," [1] in this lies the grandeur of Justinian's picture of the triumphs of the Roman Eagle. [2]

As Mr. Bryce should be read for a key to Dante's politics, so should Æneid, vi., be read as a clue to that large part of Dante's imagery which is a close working out of Virgilian suggestions.

Dante is rich enough to borrow without danger of showing poverty at home. His reproduction of Virgil's scenery is so vivid that it shows wealth of imagination, not the lack of it—his own eye for country is sufficiently seen in such passages as Guido del Duca's sketch of the Valley of the Arno, and the description given to Guido da Montefeltro of Romagna, beginning—

> " Ravenna stands as it long years hath stood ;
> The Eagle of Polenta there is brooding."

He makes us see and hear the picture that intensifies the misery of Master Adam, the forger, in his thirst—

> " The rivulets, that from the verdant hills
> Of Cassentin descend down into Arno,
> Making their channel-courses cool and soft."

Just as his eye for Nature is so true and keen that he has no need to fear comparison with Virgil's scenery, so he is able to invent incidents

[1] " Purgatorio," vi.   [2] " Paradiso," vi.

that hold their own with the most moving records he transcribes from history. The story of Ulysses and his last voyage (to which Tennyson owes so much); of the old age of Guido da Montefeltro and the logician fiend who snatched his soul from St. Francis because of the one piece of evil counsel; the companion picture in the " Purgatorio " of the son, Buonconte da Montefeltro,—so forsaken that " Giovanna nor none other cared for him," but whose soul was saved because " of one poor little tear;" the biography of Statius with its delicate homage to Virgil, who had lighted Statius to the saving Faith he failed to attain himself; these and many other such episodes show that Dante could handle with equal skill things new and old.

In the " Inferno," time is measured by the moon, the sun is never mentioned, and Dante's passion for light only shows itself by his intense perception of the " eternal shade." But on the first page of the " Purgatorio " we breathe a new atmosphere—the reader heaves a sigh of relief to find himself once more, in the pure air that had " the sweet colour of the Oriental sapphire," standing with Dante on the seashore at the foot of the Delectable Mountain. As Cato, the guardian of the mount, hears Virgil's story, the dawn of Easter Sunday breaks—

> " The dawn was vanquishing the matin hour
> Which fled before it, so that from afar
> I recognized the trembling of the sea."

The orange tints of sunrise overspread the sky while Virgil, in obedience to Cato, girds Dante with the rush of humility and cleanses his face with morning dew from the stains of the Inferno, *i.e.* from the recollection of evil that impairs the clearness of vision which is the condition of seeing God. With eyes thus "purged by euphrasy and rue," [1] Dante saw approach the bark of the Celestial Pilot, "who had a face like a Benediction." [2] More than a hundred spirits sat within, chanting *In exitu Israel*, the Psalm which Dante might have heard at Beatrice's funeral.

With this mystic chant in his ears, of the exodus from corruption to glorious liberty, Dante begins his upward road ; but more earthly music soon caused him to be "oblivious to go and make him fair." Among the newly arrived is Casella, who, in old student days in Florence, had set Dante's poems to music, "that used to quiet in him all his longings," and who now began to sing one of these same songs so melodiously. Says Dante, "The melody within me still is sounding." But the laggard souls who stayed "attentive to the note" were upbraided by Cato, with an inflexibility of judgment that showed him to belong in heart to Minos and the relentless rulers of that Inferno from which he had been set free by "the Mighty One, with sign of Victory in-coronate." The irresistible attraction for a poet,

---

[1] Milton.   [2] Don Quixote.

of hearing his own verses sung in the Spirit-world, would have been understood by the gentle warders of the Purgatorio, beings—

"Vested in white, and in their countenance
Such as appears the tremulous morning star."

But the upward path is now resumed, and, on this Easter Day, Dante meets with those who had delayed repentance till the hour of death, and who must now delay their entrance into Purgatory proper. Among them are Manfred and Buonconte, and Balacqua, the flute player of Florence, well known to Dante and Casella, "lazier than if Laziness were his sister."

These all tell their tales at length, unlike the Troubadour Sordello, who reminds us of Saladin sitting alone in the Castle of Human Wisdom—

"O Lombard soul,
How lofty and disdainful thou didst bear thee,
And grand and slow in moving of thine eyes !
Nothing whatever did it say to us,
But let us go our way, eyeing us only
After the manner of a couchant lion."

Sordello is as imperiously heedless of Virgil's words, as Farinata had been of Dante's, but the name of "Mantua" rouses him to warm affection, and to an outpouring of his own brooding grief for Italian feuds, which is repaid by Virgil, who breaks the silence of his usual proud patience to describe his own sorrow. Only once had he appealed for sympathy, when he spoke to Dante of the mighty dead who had that desire for knowledge " which evermore is given them for a grief."

> "I speak of Aristotle and Plato
> And others many ; and here he bowed his head
> And more he said not, and remained disturbed."

This was a momentary self-betrayal soon suppressed, but to Sordello he describes at length his lot in the place of sighs, where he—

> "Dwells with the little innocents
> Snatched by the teeth of Death, or ever they
> Were from our human sinfulness exempt."

Nightfall comes on, and Sordello guides them to the Valley of the Princes,—rulers who, owing to the honourable occupation of governing their kingdoms, gave too little heed to their own spiritual condition.

The "herbage and the flowers within that hollow" are painted with all the colours of Giotto's pre-Raphaelite paint-box—

> "Nor in that place had nature painted only,
> But of the sweetness of a thousand odours
> Made there a mingled fragrance and unknown."

Seated on the green and flowers, spirits were singing *Salve Regina*, the compline hymn of exiles.

Among them was Rudolph the Emperor, with the semblance " of having what he should have done neglected," and Harry of England, " monarch of the simple life."

But the sweetest singer and the most devout, was Judge Nino of Sardinia, kneeling (as Dante may have often seen him in life), with hands devoutly joined, as the Angelus bell sounded—

> " At the hour that turneth back desire,
>   In those who sail the sea, and melts the heart,
>   The day they've said to their sweet friends farewell."

" Fixing his eyes upon the Orient, as if he said to God, ' Naught else I care for,' " he sang the compline hymn, *Te lucis ante*, so sweetly, that Dante's whole soul was joined with his. Night falls on this noble company, and Dante sleeps; awakened by the twittering of the swallows, he finds that he had been carried in his sleep up to the Gate of Purgatory. Here he ascends the three steps, the polished white marble of Self-knowledge, the black granite of Confession, and the flaming porphyry of the Blood of the Atonement.

The warder of the gate, with the golden key of Authority, and the silver key of Discernment, admitted Dante, tracing on his brow seven " P's," emblematic of the seven Peccata, or sins, from which he must be purged.

Thus, early on Easter Monday, Dante enters on the first circle of Purgatory, where the Proud are " purging away the smoke-stains of the world," bent by such burdens—

" That he who had most patience in his looks,
    Weeping did seem to say, ' I can no more.' "

As they passed by, the Lord's Prayer comes from
their lips, in a paraphrase where we seem to over-
hear the private prayers of Dante himself. It is
like the stern, sad wanderer, described in Fra
Ilario's letter, to render " Thy Kingdom come,"
by the words—

" Come unto us the peace of Thy Dominion,
    For unto it we cannot of ourselves,
    If it come not, with all our intellect."

On the pathway beneath their feet are sculptured
scenes so life-like that we remember how Dante
may have been a fellow-student with Giotto in the
studio of Cimabue, and learnt there to appreciate
the art which could depict Gabriel so truthfully.

" There sculptured in a gracious attitude,
    He did not seem an image that is silent.
    One could have sworn that he was saying 'Ave.' "

Further on, the " image of Michal glimmered
white upon him," and then came the scene in
Trajan's life, of that deed of patient justice to the
widow, which earned him future salvation through
the prayers of Pope Gregory. In all these scenes
" dead seemed the dead, the living seemed alive."

Dante's artistic sympathies are also roused by
meeting Oderisi, " honour of that art which is in

Paris called illuminating," with whom Dante talks feelingly of the fickleness of literary fame.

The Angel who now meets them brushed Dante's forehead with his pinion, erasing the P which stood for Pride. Dante, in his new-born humility, is unconscious of this, and wonders at the greater easiness of the ascent. Virgil tells him that when all his sins are purged away—

> " His feet will be so vanquished by good will,
> That not alone they shall not feel fatigue,
> But urging up will be to them delight."

They now pass upwards to the Terrace of the Envious, to whom Dante shows special courtesy, perhaps because he is so free from all touch of their failing that he pities from his heart those who are labelled with a fault so odious to a proud nature like his own.

These souls are sitting disconsolately with blind eyes, in sackcloth coloured like the stone they sit on. To Dante's courteous nature—

> "It seemed in passing, to do outrage,
> Seeing the others without being seen."

So he addresses them, with a deference he shows to no one else, saying, "O people, certain of beholding the full glory of that light which alone you wish for." He asks if any Latian is among them, but the souls have risen above the earthly jealousies, so strong in Italy, to the thought of the

Heavenly Jerusalem, " the Rome where Christ is a
Roman," and he is answered—

> " O brother mine, each one is citizen
> Of the one true city."

Local feelings are not extinct, however, for in
the next canto (xiv.) Guido del Duca gives an
account of the Valley of the Arno and its inhabi-
tants, with a bitterness which makes Ampère call it
" a piece of topographical satire, of which I know
no other example."

Dante now ascends to the next terrace, while
" Blessed are the Merciful " was sung behind him.
Each terrace has one of the Beatitudes assigned
to it for a song of triumph when souls ascend to
the next stage, and compassion for misfortune is
chosen as the one cure for envy.

He now reaches the Terrace of Anger.   Here,
and here only in Purgatory, he finds thick fog, for
to be conscious of anger is to be in Hell with all its
darkness.   Dante must have felt that thick mist of
rage within him, when he wrote the previous canto
on the Arno ; and his letter to Henry VII. about
the sins of the Florentines, one long fierce invective,
was written about the same time, so he spoke from
experience.   He kept close to Virgil (or human
wisdom)—

> " E'en as a blind man goes behind his guide,
> Lest he should wander, or should strike against

> Aught that may harm or peradventure kill him,
> So I went through the bitter and foul air."

But he knows that the only true remedy is to be found in the *Agnus Dei*, which is the prayer of all around him. In this terrace, teaching is conveyed in visions instead of in sculpture, in order to develop the contemplative side, deficient in the wrathful. Among the scenes so revealed is a picture of St. Stephen, "who of his eyes made ever gates to Heaven," and "in the din of so great a battle" implored the high Lord to pardon his foes. Virgil, who knows the implacable rancour of a Florentine, here, and here only, enforces the lesson—

> " What thou hast seen was that thou mayst not fail
> To ope thy heart unto the waters of peace."

Then, to the music of "*Beati Pacifici*, who are without ill-anger," Dante mounts to the Terrace of Accidie, where—

> "The love of good, remiss
> In what it should have done, is here restored ;
> Here plied again the ill-belated oar."

It is curious that no prayer is assigned to these souls ; perhaps in their slothful lives they had lost the faculty of prayer. As usual they are urged on by alternate Biblical and Classical examples. The souls who run round this terrace are urged to haste by hearing of Mary hastening to Hebron, and of Cæsar hastening to conquer Spain, while their upward course is cheered by the Beatitude, "Blessed are they that mourn, for their souls shall be Queens of Consolation." "The essence of Accidie is a shrinking from effort. He who accepts that pain, shall have a soul, mistress of every true element of consolation."[1] In the next circle of avarice, Dante finds Pope Adrian V., whose noble nature had learnt through success the lesson of humility, which a smaller nature would have found only in humiliation. Elevation to the highest earthly dignities opened his eyes to his own meaner nature, and made him realize that his "eye did not uplift itself aloft, being fastened upon earthly things."

Hugh Capet then gives so long a history of the future sins of his descendants, that Benvenuto, the early commentator on Dante, says at the end, "And there really was not time for talking any more in this twentieth canto, which contains in itself so many noble histories, fictions, and opinions." The talk is interrupted by an earthquake, which is the thrill of joy felt by the whole mountain when any soul ascends to a higher terrace. Statius, the poet, was the cause in this instance, and he joins Dante and Virgil, in like manner, "that Christ appeared to two upon the way." He tells how the Æneid had been his "nurse in song," and says that, to see Virgil, he would accept an added year of Purgatory. Virgil turned to Dante, "with looks that in their

[1] Plumptre.

silence said, Ee silent!'" Dante smiled, and
Statius gazed "into his eyes, where most expression dwells," saying—

> " Why did thy face just now
>   Display to me the lightning of a smile?"

The talk that follows, when Dante makes his
favourite writers known to each other, expresses the
most delicate hero-worship ever conceived. Virgil
marvels that Statius, a heathen, should be bound
for Paradise instead of Limbo, and Statius replies
to him, "Through thee I poet was, through thee a
Christian." Dante gives an ideal biography of
Statius, without authority, and describes what he
thinks must have been the effect of the Virgilian
prophecy in the Fourth Eclogue, putting his own
reverence for Virgil into the mouth of Statius.
When the latter asks for news of his heathen friends,
Virgil describes those dwelling in Limbo, "among
whom some of thine own people may be seen."
It must have been sweet to Statius to hear his own
poems quoted by his master, and they walked on,
deep in talk that gave Dante " lessons in the art of
song."

Now comes the Terrace of Gluttony, where Dante
finds his brother-in-law, Forese Donati, who says he
is thus far advanced in Purgatory because—

> " My Nella, with her overflowing tears,
>   She with her prayers devout and with her sighs
>   Has from the other circles set me free."

The next soul they meet salutes Dante as author of the canzone, "Ladies, that have intelligence of Love." As Dante quotes it elsewhere, we may conclude it was his own favourite, and that it was dear to his soul, even though purged of pride, to find it thus loved in the spirit world.

Then comes the guiding voice of the Angel of Abstinence, "This way goes he who goeth after peace." A fresh breeze here symbolizes the "clear brightness and sweetness of the temperate life "—

> " And as, the harbinger of early dawn,
> The air of May doth move and breathe out fragrance,
> Impregnate all with herbage and with flowers,
> So did I feel a breeze strike in the midst
> My front, and felt the moving of the plumes
> That breathed around an odour of ambrosia."

The heavenly choir now sing, from the Vulgate, the Beatitude, " Blessed are they which hunger and thirst righteously," *i.e.* whose higher nature rules their lower one.

Now comes the last terrace, where Impurity is cleansed by a fire so fierce that Dante's shadow, falling on it, makes the flame appear more red, a description of fire which Ruskin says is the finest known.

Then comes one of the many passages of the " Purgatorio " that make the tenderness of Dante transfuse all his sternness. Virgil cannot induce his

N

pupil to brave the flames which are necessary to fit
him for Paradise, until he says—

> " Now look thou, Son,
>   'Twixt Beatrice and thee there is this wall."

Dante turned to his " wise Guide, who smiled
as one doth at a child who's vanquished by an
apple." Twice before had Virgil smiled—when the
four great Poets had adopted Dante as one of
themselves, and when Dante was purged from his
besetting sin of pride. He smiles now with the
generous sweetness of a noble nature at seeing how
much stronger than his own was another's influence
over this " Son," to whom he had so devoted
himself. He was to smile once more with the
same self-forgetful sweetness in hearing Matilda
describe the joys that were not destined to be
his.

The flames were hotter than molten glass—

> " But my sweet Father, to encourage me,
>   Discoursing still of Beatrice, went on,
>   Saying, ' Her eyes I seem to see already!' "

When they attain the next and final staircase, night
falls, and they rest on the stairs, a companion
picture to the twilight scene in the Valley of the
Princes. As goats upon the mountains, hushed
in the shadow while the sun is hot, are watched

---

1 " Purgatorio," xxviii. 146.

by the herdsman, who upon his staff is leaning,
and in leaning tendeth them—

> "Such at that hour were we, all three of us,
> I like the goat, and like the herdsmen they,
> Begirt on this side and on that by rocks,
> Little could there be seen of things without ;
> But through that little I beheld the stars,
> More luminous and larger than their wont."

Watching his beloved stars, sleep seized upon him,
and he dreamt of Leah plucking a garland to
adorn herself, and of Rachel gazing in her mirror,
—types, says Ruskin, " of unglorified (because self-
ending) Action and Contemplation. Matilda and
Beatrice are the same temperaments glorified,
because centred in God."

The dream fled as Easter Wednesday dawned,
the day on which "rejoicing came the beauteous
eyes," " whose weeping had brought Virgil unto
him."

Dante has now been purged from the Seven Sins,
and Virgil knows that his work is done, that Dante's
nature is now cleansed and healed, and needs only
to be spiritualized by the Beatific Vision. This
higher life cannot be shared by Virgil ; he belongs
to the noble company of " friends of the bride-
groom," to Jonathan and John the Baptist, and
many another finely tempered soul, which has
learnt to rejoice in seeing another fill their own niche
in life. Dante has been as Virgil's own child

throughout the journey; it was the touch of his
hand which alone nerved Dante to enter the
infernal regions. When the demons of Malebolge
threatened, we read—

> "My Leader on a sudden seized me up,
> Even as a mother who by noise is wakened,
> And close beside her sees the enkindled flames,
> Who takes her son, and flies, and does not stop,
> Having more care of him than of herself,
> So that she clothes her only with a shift.
> So did my Master down along that border,
> Bearing me with him on his breast away,
> As his own son, and not as a companion."

Virgil reads Dante's inmost thoughts so instan-
taneously that he says—

> "Were I a mirror,
> Thine outward image I should not attract,
> Sooner to me than I imprint the inner."

"Well knew he," says Dante, later on, "what the
mute one wished to say;" and half-regretfully,
at the beginning of their friendship, Dante had
exclaimed—

> "Ah me! how very cautious men should be
> With those who not alone behold the act,
> But with their wisdom look into their thoughts."

But his love is stern as a cleansing fire, when Dante
listens to the quarrel between Master Adam and
Sinon, he is roused by a look and tone from Virgil
that made him turn away—

> " With such shame
> That still it eddies through his memory."

His speechless shame so touched his Master that he is forgiven : " Less shame doth wash away a greater fault."

> " But make account that I am aye beside thee,
> If e'er it come to pass that fortune bring thee
> Where there are people in a like dispute ;
> For a base wish it is to wish to hear it."

He comforts Dante in his many terrors, so that he turns to him with that reliance—

> " With which the little child runs to his mother,
> When he has fear, or when he is in grief."

But he ever rouses him to more strenuous effort—

> " Think that this day will never dawn again.
> The heavens are calling you, and wheel around you,
> Displaying to you their eternal beauties
> And still your eye is looking on the ground."

When Dante listens complacently to the interest expressed in him by passing souls, the Master's stern voice breaks in—

> " Come after me, and let the people talk ;
> Stand like a steadfast tower, that never wags
> Its summit for the blowing of the winds."

Dante is instantly—

> " With that colour tinged
> Which makes a man of pardon sometimes worthy,"

For if Virgil is a perfect master, Dante is a perfect pupil. We see him eager to learn, prompt to respond to his master's every look and tone. We see him, with " his head bowed as one who goeth reverently," in his conversation with Brunetto Latini, his old tutor, who must have had high hopes of him as a boy, for he says—

> " If thou thy star do follow,
> Thou canst not fail thee of a glorious port,
> If well I judged in the life beautiful."

Dante tells Brunetto that he bears in his heart—

> " The dear and good paternal image
> Of you, when in the world from hour to hour
> You taught me how a man becomes eternal."

Few lesson-books have been so canonized by grateful pupils as was the one written by Brunetto, whose last words are those of an author. " Commended unto thee be my Tesoro." We can fancy Brunetto's pleasure in his pupil when we watched the eager thirst for learning Dante shows in his talks with Virgil. Dante's whole nature grows and deepens as the poem proceeds, and the credit is all given to his " lofty Teacher." He is too reverent to praise him directly, but we can see his own feelings in the awestruck homage of Sordello and Statius, and we should note the beauty and delicacy of his implied farewell, when Virgil fades away before Beatrice, as the morning star before the sun.

All the songs of the angelic choir are from the Psalms or the Church Service, except at the moment of Virgil's departure. Then a line from the Æneid bursts from "the ministers and messengers of life eternal" in the act of scattering flowers to greet the Queen of Heaven. "Bring lilies here, in handfuls bring."

Virgil vanishes just as Beatrice is about to appear. The last words he hears of the heavenly song, are his own words of sorrow for Marcellus, in the use of which Dante scatters flowers over the grave which is to separate himself and Virgil. Virgil's last spoken words are the blessing he pronounces on Dante when the seven circles have been surmounted—

> "Free and upright and sound is thy free will,
> An error were it not to do its bidding:
> So, crowned and mitred, o'er thyself rule thou."

Dante is now ready for the Terrestrial Paradise, whose forest is a reminiscence of the Pineta at Ravenna, where the little birds upon the pines, singing their matin song with holy exultation, receive the first breezes of the day in the midst of leaves "that ever bore a burden to their rhymes." Through this ancient forest of the Garden of Eden sweeps the mystical pageant of Christ and His Church, beside the river of Lethe. An advance guard of the seven Spirits of God flame as a torch, and paint the air as they pass, leaving a rainbow of

sevenfold colour to mark their track. Then came
the four-and-twenty elders, "incoronate with fleur
de luce," figuring the books of the Old Testament:
then came the four living creatures of Ezekiel,
the Evangelists, and then the Car of the Church
drawn by Christ, typified by the Gryfon, with its
double nature of eagle and lion. On the left hand
of the car dance the four maidens, vested in
purple, who represent Prudence, Justice, Tem-
perance, and Fortitude—the "four consecrated"
stars by which Dante had steered his course, till he
came to the Mount of Purgatory and was guided
by the influence of the three maidens dancing
on the right hand of the Car—Faith, Hope, and
Charity, the theological virtues.

Behind the car came St. Luke, the beloved
Physician, and St. Paul the Persecutor, with a
shining sword. Then come the four writers of the
remaining Epistles, "of humble aspect," "and,
behind all, an aged man alone," St. John of the
Apocalypse, "walking in sleep with countenance
acute." These last seven writers burnt more with
love than those of the Old Testament, so, in place
of fleur de luce, their brows were bound with
roses, till,

> "At little distance would the sight have sworn
> That all were in a flame above their brows."

Having described the procession of the sacred
writers, who surrounded the Car of the Church,

Dante now tells us of Divine Wisdom, typified by the lady "vested in colour of the living flame." It was forty years since he had seen Beatrice as a little girl in the crimson dress: it was twenty-four years since she had died, and he had resolved "to speak no more of that Blessed One until he could more worthily treat of her." His hope then was "to say of her what was never said of any other woman," and that time was now come.

"From the first day that he beheld her face in this world, to the moment of her divinest smile in Paradise, the sequence of his life was never severed," [1] and he was now to describe her increasing beauty in sphere after sphere of Paradise, until she leaves him to sit on her eternal throne beside Rachel and Lucia. In Virgil he had found the perfect friend "who seeth and uprightly wills and loves;" he was now to pass into the keeping of "the Lady fair who made him strong for Heaven," and "from a slave should bring him into freedom."

Dante is borne upwards with a swiftness at which he marvels, till Beatrice—

> "After a pitying sigh,
> Her eyes directed towards me with that look
> A mother casts on a delirious child,"

and with a "few brief words, more smiled than spoken," told him that, now he is purified from sin, it would be as great a marvel were he not so to

[1] Plumptre.

rise " as if on earth the living fire were quiet." It
is natural for the child of God to ascend in heart
and mind : the marvel to Beatrice is that men are
so often like Mammon, " with looks downwards
bent " ! [1]

In this first Heaven, that of the Moon, Dante
finds those whose perfection had been marred by
weakness of will.   His scientific mind is exercised
by the question of lunar spots, and Beatrice sets his
doubts at rest by a long discourse which is chiefly
interesting to us for the light it throws on Dante's
mind. Here, as in Statius' discourse on embryology
in Purg. xxv., we see Dante fascinated by the new
theory of his day. Roger Bacon was the only
other physicist of the time who held the theory
Dante assigns to Beatrice, so that we probably find
here a personal remembrance of the great Englishman, who had been Dante's friend in his student
days at Paris.

In the heaven of the Moon Dante is encompassed
by a luminous cloud.

> " Into itself did the eternal pearl
>   Receive us, even as water doth receive
>   A ray of light."

In these crystalline depths was a vision of fair
faces, " seen faintly as a pearl on forehead white."
He speaks to one of these spirits, who, " with laughing eyes," bids him recognize in her, Piccarda, his

[1] " Paradise Lost."

wife's sister. He courteously excuses his non-recognition of her, saying—

> "In your miraculous aspects
> There shines I know not what of the Divine,
> Therefore I was not swift in my remembrance."

He asks her if her happiness is disturbed by wishes for a higher place—whether she and her fellows are disquieted by any wish to drink more deeply of the two great sources in the joy of Paradise, the Beatific Vision and the Communion of Saints.

> " ' But tell me, ye who in this place are happy,
> Are you desirous of a higher place,
> To see more or to make yourselves more friends?'
> First with those other shades she smiled a little;
> Thereafter answered me so full of gladness,
> She seemed to burn in the first fire of love:
> ' Brother, our will is quieted by virtue
> Of charity, that makes us wish alone
> For what we have, nor gives us thirst for more.
> If to be more exalted we aspired,
> Discordant would our aspirations be
> Unto the will of Him who here secludes us;
> . . . 'Tis essential to this blest existence
> To keep itself within the will Divine,
> Whereby our very wishes are made one;
> So that our station to all the realm is pleasing,
> As to the King, who makes His will our will,
> And His will is our peace.' "

She tells him how, when a Poor Clare, she was torn from the sweet cloister by her brothers: "'God knows what afterwards my life became.'"

"The outline is left to be filled up. Remorse, endurance, asceticism, prayers to depart may all be included in these words, as full of meaning as the story of La Pia, in Purg. v. 133."[1]

Beside Piccarda is Constance, mother of Frederick II., who was "to the world returned against her wishes," though " of the heart's veil she never was divested."

It seems hard to Dante that these fair souls should suffer through the wrong of others, but Beatrice explains that they should have returned as soon as they were free, "for will is never quenched unless it will." She believes, with Bunyan's Mr. Honest, that "a Christian can never be overcome, unless he should yield himself," and she laments that "a solid will is all too rare."

They now enter the Second Heaven of Mercury.

> " The little planet which adorns itself
> With the good spirits that have active been,
> That fame and honour might come after them."

Here dwell the great lawgivers, a characteristic part of whose joy is to measure their wages by their desert, and to admire the just proportions of the Divine Law.

Here Justinian unrolls before Dante a picture of the course of the Roman eagle, symbol of that empire which was, to Dante, God manifest in the

[1] Plumptre.

world; and Beatrice, "lighting him with a smile such
as would make one happy in the fire," treats of the
doctrine of the Atonement in one of those passages
which show Dante as fulfilling Westcott's definition
of a perfect theologian : " a perfect scholar, a perfect
physicist, and a perfect philosopher."

In the Heaven of Venus he is greeted by a line
of the canzone in which he himself, in his youthful
days at Florence, sang the praises of the angels
who move in this Third Heaven.

Perhaps the line was suggested to the celestial
choir by the friend of his youth who now speaks to
him. This is Charles Martel, who had made friends
with Dante—some ten years his senior—when
he stayed at Florence as a boy of twenty-two.
Dante may have seen in this heir to Provence,
Naples, Hungary, and Sicily, the Righteous Ruler
whom he afterwards sought in Henry VII.; but
Charles died in the following year, and Dante's
next sight of him must have been here in Paradise,
"rayed round and hidden by his own gladness,
like a silk worm swathed in its own silk."

The Heaven of Venus has many reminders of
past days in Florence, for close to Charles stands
Cunizza, who loved Sordello, married the astrologer
of her brother Ezzelin, and ended her days in
Florence as a devout and gracious lady, retaining
her dazzling beauty even in old age. She made
her will in the house of Guido Cavalcanti's father,

the year Dante was born, so that Guido, then a boy of sixteen, may have told Dante of her pious and charitable old age.

In the Heaven of the Sun Dante sees "Lights many, vivid and triumphant." These are the souls of theologians, among whom is pre-eminent Thomas Aquinas the most learned of saints and the most holy of learned men. He is the patron saint of teachers; and well he may be, for he always sought for light in his studies by prayer, and said that he learnt more in prayer at the foot of his crucifix than from any book. His "Summa Theologicæ" was intended to collect the writing of the Fathers and doctors of the Church, during the preceding twelve centuries, and to build them up in one great body of Christian doctrine. This great work, so carefully studied by Dante, was the only book of reference, except the Bible, used at the Council of Trent; and when St. Thomas was canonized by Pope John XXII. and it was objected that he had worked few miracles during his life, the Pope replied, that every article of the "Summa" was in itself a miracle. His vast learning was only equalled by his humility. Once when a student at Paris, he was reading aloud in the refectory. The superior corrected him wrongly; and, with great humility, he adopted the false quantity. On the other brothers expressing surprise afterwards, he said, "It matters little how a

word is pronounced, but much to practise humility
and obedience."

We no longer read the "Summa," but St.
Thomas's prayers still express our needs : "May
all labour delight me which is for Thee, and all
rest be weariness which is not in Thee." "Grant
me diligence in study, quickness of apprehension,
and power to retain what I learn." "Grant that I
may never desire to do what is unwise, and that
I may never be discouraged in what is distasteful ;
that I may never begin my works before the proper
time, nor abandon them before they are completed. Amen."

Dante must have been in full sympathy with St.
Thomas, who used to pray, "Give me, O Lord, a
noble heart which no earthly affection can drag
down ;" and we can imagine his pleasure when his
master introduced him to the great teachers of the
schools, Albertus Magnus, "the Universal Doctor ;"
Peter Lombard, "Master of Sentences ;" Gratian,
the monk of St. Apollinare in Classe at Ravenna,
who is still an authority on Canon Law. With
these, was Boethius, who "from martyrdom and
banishment came unto this peace," and whose
"Consolations of Philosophy" had helped strengthen
Dante when Beatrice died. St. Thomas tells the
story of St. Francis of Assisi, and his friend St.
Bonaventura tells the story of St. Dominic, "the
zealous lover of the Christian Faith, the athlete

consecrate," who "went about that vineyard, which fadeth soon if faithless be the dresser."

In the fifth Heaven of Mars, the flames, in which dwell souls of Crusaders, form a Greek cross, and the lights shoot from arm to arm of the cross—

" As through the pure and tranquil evening air
    There shoots from time to time a sudden fire,
    And seems to be a star that changeth place."

One of these stars ran to the cross's foot, and, greeting Dante in words of antique sound, proved to be his ancestor Cacciaguida, who "came from martydom unto this peace." Beatrice, who knows every thought of Dante's heart, and, " saw his silentness in the light of Him who seeth everything," knows well his pride in "the poor nobility of blood" and sympathizes with it; for when Dante turned to her for leave to speak, he saw burning in her eyes such a smile—

" That with mine own methought I touched the bottom,
    Both of my grace and of my Paradise ! "

Then follows a long tale, in which Dante listens with delight to accounts of old days in Florence and of his own ancestry and their dwelling-place. His belief in heredity often appears in the poem, so that we may feel this talk solved for him some of the problems of his own life, besides gratifying that pride of birth to which he reads a lesson on *noblesse oblige* and the duty of maintaining family traditions—

" O thou, our poor nobility of blood,
Truly thou art a cloak that quickly shortens,
So that, unless we piece thee day by day,
Time goeth round thee with his shears ! "

Cacciaguida foretells to Dante the banishment awaiting him :—

" Thou shalt abandon everything beloved
Most tenderly,
Thou shalt have proof how savoureth of salt
The bread of others, and how hard a road
The going down and up another's stairs."

In times past, Virgil had exhorted Dante to—

" Stand like a stedfast tower, that never wags
Its summit for the blowing of the winds."

He has learnt the lesson now, and, as he says, can "stand foursquare against the blows of chance ; " but he shrinks from the thought of faithfully reporting, to the great ones upon earth, the adverse judgments pronounced against so many of them in the courts of Heaven.

Cacciaguida tells him it is no slight argument of honour to be chosen " to smite, as doth the wind, the most exalted summits ; " and " the lady who to God was leading him," reminds him that " He who lightens every wrong is at her side."

" Unto the loving accents of my comfort I turned me, and her fair face conquered me with the radiance of a smile, so that my heart from every baser longing was released." His courage

O

was further heightened by a vision of heroes, whose souls " flashed athwart the Cross," Joshua the great Maccabee, Charlemagne, Duke Godfrey, Robert Guisoard,—a sight so dear to Beatrice that I beheld her eyes—

> " So full of pleasure, that her countenance
> Surpassed its other and its latest wont."

In the sixth Heaven of Jupiter, the home of Justice, the souls, " like birds uprisen from the shore, made squadrons of themselves," and, forming with their flames the words " Diligite justitiam qui judicatis terram," remained in the *m* of the last word, so arranged that " Jupiter seemed to be silver there inlaid with gold." As Dante gazed on the illumination the *m* changed shape, and he beheld the head of an eagle " delineated by that inlaid fire."

Dante turns to this incarnation of Justice to solve the doubt, " which was in him so very old a fast."

The doubt is, How can it be consistent with justice that a virtuous heathen should be condemned? The eagle convinces him that the Divine judgments are far above out of his sight, so that he lifted grateful eyes to his teacher, even as when above—

> " The nest goes circling round
> The stork when she has fed her little ones,
> And he who has been fed looks up at her."

This answer is enforced when he is shown the chief rulers who form the eagle's head, for not only does he see David, Hezekiah, and Constantine, but two heathens, Trajan the Emperor, and Ripheus, noted by Virgil as the most just among the Trojans and most obedient to the right. Trajan, when recalled to life for a brief hour by Pope Gregory's prayer, kindled to such fire of love that, at its close, " in His unerring sight Who measures life by love," [1] he was thought worthy of the joy of Paradise. Ripheus set all his love below on righteousness, wherefore God " revealed to him redemption yet to be, and Faith, Hope, and Charity,—

" Those Maidens three, whom at the right-hand wheel
Thou didst behold, were unto him for baptism
More than a thousand years before baptizing."

This revelation of the mercy of God put Dante yet more in tune with the heavenly choir, who sang " that whatsoever God wills we also will."

He was now uplifted to the " seventh splendour," Saturn, the Heaven of Contemplation, where he saw the symbol of the contemplative life, the mystic ladder " coloured like gold on which the sunshine gleams," where angels descend and prayers ascend. Here the corruption of the Church is denounced by St. Benedict and by St. Peter Damiano, monk of Sta. Maria in Porto Fuori at Ravenna, where Dante wrote these cantos.

Dante now rises to the Heaven of the Fixed

[1] Keble.

Stars, and sees Beatrice, erect and vigilant, with expectant gaze.

> " Even as a bird, 'mid the beloved leaves,
>   Quiet upon the nest of her sweet brood
>   Throughout the night, that hideth all things from us,
>   Who, that she may behold their longed-for looks,
>   And find the food wherewith to nourish them,
>   In which, to her, grave labours grateful are,
>   Anticipates the time on open spray,
>   And with an ardent longing waits the sun,
>   Gazing intent as soon as breaks the dawn."

Then came the vision of Christ's triumphal march, and Beatrice prays the "company elect to the great supper of the Lamb benedight," to satisfy Dante's "immense desire" for knowledge. At this there "issues forth a fire so happy that none it left there of a greater brightness;" for joy in Paradise is shown by greater light, even as, on earth, by smiles. This happy soul is St. Peter, who subjects Dante to an examination on Faith, which must have reminded him of baccalaureate days in Paris and Oxford. He acquitted himself so well that "the Baron," St. Peter, gave him a triple benediction. This crowning honour in Paradise recalled to him the earthly honour which he was to crave in vain, the laurel crown of his "fair sheepfold," Florence. The hope flashes across his mind that perhaps the poem—

> " To which both heaven and earth have set their hand,
>   So that it many a year hath made me lean,"

may win him entrance to that city which is as
near his heart as it was in the " Inferno," though
less often on his tongue.

Then comes St. James to examine Dante on
Hope, and—

> " In the same way as, when a dove alights
> Near his companion, both of them pour forth,
> Circling about and murmuring, their affection,
> So one beheld I by the other grand
> Prince glorified to be with welcome greeted."

St. James says that what—

> " Comes hither from the mortal world,
> Must needs be ripened in our radiance ; "

and surely Dante has been so ripened, for it must
have needed all the light and hope, with which
every line of the " Paradiso" is instinct, to teach
such a nature as Dante's that Hope is the chief
mark " of all the souls whom God hath made His
friends."

Dante was by nature one of those who most
often sojourn in the "melancholy inn" of Jacob
Böhme ; but Beatrice, who knows him through and
through, answers for him unhesitatingly, that the
" Church Militant possesses no child more full of
hope : " he had surely learnt it " close at her side,
and in the Happy World."

St. John now questions him on love, and Adam
tells him of the life in Eden, the primeval soul

being "so jubilant to give him pleasure" that it
thrilled through its covering of light, even as a cat's
vibrations of pleasure are seen under the wrappage
of its fur. Dante now ascends to the Primum
Mobile, the sphere which surrounded all the others
and set them all in motion. As he passes upward
he looks to the homeward "great vision of the
guarded mount" and the mad track of Ulysses ; but
the vision of the world was as nothing compared
to the divine delight of gazing on Beatrice, who
"imparadised his mind" and—

> "Smiled so joyously,
> That God's own joy seemed in her face to dwell."

She satisfies his curiosity about the angels with an
answer which was clearer to him than to us ; for
as the west wind drives away the clouds—

> "Till the welkin laughs
> With all the beauties of its pageantry ;
> Thus did I likewise, after that my Lady
> Had me provided with her clear response,
> And like a star in heaven the truth was seen."

They now ascend to the Empyrean, the highest
Heaven, the motionless home of God Himself,
"The Love which quieteth this Heaven." His
Lady's beauty has increased at every nearer
approach to the presence of God, and now—

> "If what has hitherto been said of her
> Were all concluded in a single praise
> Scant would it be to serve the present turn."

Dante's mind lost all power at the mere "memory of that sweet smile," when with "voice and gesture of a perfect leader," she told him of the vision he was about to behold of the hosts of Paradise, clothed in those bodies which would not be theirs till the Judgment Day. In the Theologian's Heaven Dante had been troubled by doubts as to whether even the resurrection body could bear the radiance of the light of Heaven. The saints had reassured him, saying—

> " ' So great a splendour cannot weary us,
> For strong will be the organs of the body
> To everything which hath the power to please us.'
> So sudden and alert appeared to me
> Both one and the other choir to say Amen,
> That well they showed desire for their dead bodies ;
> Nor sole for them perhaps, but for the mothers,
> The fathers, and the rest who had been dear
> Or ever they became eternal flames."

Dante's first vision in the Empyrean was of the River of the Grace of God. Its banks were rich with all the flowers of spring, the souls of saints.

> " Out of this river issued living sparks,
> And on all sides sank down into the flowers,
> Like unto rubies that are set in gold,"—

these topaz and ruby sparks being the angels in ministry of joy and fellowship.

As he gazes, the vision changes into a mystic Rose mirrored in that divine river as a hill mirrors its flowers and "laughing herbage" in the lake at its foot.

Beatrice bids him note "how vast the convent of the white stoles," and how a throne is waiting for the noble Henry who should try in vain to redress the wrongs of Italy. Her last words are a cry for vengeance on Clement V., the Pope whose double dealing had frustrated Henry's hopes of regenerating the world.

It is a shock to us that her last words should be political, not spiritual: but to Dante politics were the building of the City of God on earth, and it may well have harmonized, in his mind, that the last words of her who was his inspiration all through life, should be concerned with the hero round whom his latest hopes turned, the Emperor whom he had believed to be the one who should have redeemed God's Israel.

Beatrice returns to her own place, and as Dante prays her still to help his soul which she has healed, she, so far away,—

> " Smiled, as it seemed, and looked once more at me ;
> Then unto the eternal fountain turned."

But St. Bernard was now to guide Dante to still higher love. "As Aquinas mastered men's intellects, so Bernard of Clairvaux mastered their hearts," and he used his power to spread devotion to the Queen of Heaven. Dean Plumptre, in his notes on Dante, to which I am so much indebted, attributes much of the honour paid to her by the hymns, paintings, and lady-chapels of the twelfth, thirteenth, and fourteenth centuries, to the influence of St. Bernard's sermons.

Dante, who had "been made strong for Heaven" by the smile of Beatrice, now finally and indelibly learns the lesson she and Virgil had so laboured to teach him; he learns it in the smile of the Blessed Virgin, "which makes glad with fullest joy the eyes of all the other saints in Paradise:" he learns that—

> " Before that Light one grows to such content
> That to turn back from it to aught beside
> The soul can never possibly consent.''

POETS.

Chaucer's Prologue.

Shakspeare's Hamlet, Macbeth, Lear, Julius Cæsar, King John, Henry V., Merchant of Venice, As You Like It, Much Ado about Nothing.

Spenser's Faery Queen.

George Herbert.

Henry Vaughan.

Milton.

Pope's Essay on Man.

Gray.

Goldsmith.

Cowper.
Coleridge.
Wordsworth.
Scott.
Byron's "Childe Harold."
Mrs. Hemans.
"Dream of Gerontius."
Tennyson. 7*s*. 6*d*.
Selections from Robert Browning and Mrs. Browning.
Trench. 7*s*. 6*d*.
Matthew Arnold. 7*s*. 6*d*.
Clough. 7*s*. 6*d*.
Legendary Ballads of Scotland and England.
Palgrave's Golden Treasury.
      ,,   Treasury of Sacred Poetry. 4*s*. 6*d*.
Dante, translated by Longfellow (or Plumptre. *s*. *h*.)
Molière's Bourgeois Gentilhomme, L'Avare, Les Femmes
    Savantes, Le Misanthrope.
Goethe's Ballads and Torquato Tasso and Iphigenia.
Schiller's Ballads and Wallenstein.
Uhland's Ballads.
Longfellow.
Lowell.
Whittier.
Keats.

(Except where otherwise specified, the cost is 2*s*. 6*d*. or
under.)

III.

" Lord, with what care hast Thou begirt us round !
    Parents first season us : then schoolmasters
    Deliver us to laws ; they send us bound
  To rules of reason, holy messengers,
  Pulpits and Sundays."

GEORGE HERBERT.

Sunday Reading.

SUNDAY reading means very different things in different households. Some people think everything wrong except sermons, others make no difference from their weekday reading. I should not like to say that a book which is good and wholesome reading on Saturday night, becomes a sin on Sunday morning. Very possibly, as Dr. Arnold says, St. Paul, could he return among us, would be shocked to find us still needing to keep Sunday. But his point of view would be that, after so many years of grace, all our days ought to be—

> " Bracelets to adorn the wife
> Of the Eternal Glorious King."

If we read as many spiritual books on weekdays as we need for our souls' health, there would be no necessity for any "Sunday reading." But most of us do not so spend our weekdays, and it is therefore at our souls' peril that we reject each Sunday's offer of a "truce of God" with the cares and labours of the weekday life—

" When each day brings its petty dust,
    Our soon choked souls to fill." [1]

Practically, if we do not read good books on Sundays, we do not read them at all; it is not so much that a novel is wrong on Sunday, as that better things leave no time for it. In this, as in all else, it is not a negative rule which should keep us right, but, " the expulsive power of a new affection." [2]

If Sunday reading be considered merely from the point of view of one whose main wish is to improve his mind, it has overwhelming claims; for it comprises the grandest half of that heritage of English literature with which such an one seeks to be acquainted. Milton, Jeremy Taylor, Keble, Bunyan, Henry Vaughan, George Herbert, Newman, quite apart from their bearing on the spiritual life, must be studied by any one who would know " the best that has been thought and said."

In taking the matter from a higher point of view, there are two special blessings for which we might advantageously seek in our Sunday reading—enthusiasm, and sympathy with those who differ from us.

Some start with more, some with less enthusiasm; but contact with the world rubs off so much from every one, that, as Hare says,[3] every mother should seek to equip her son in a three-pile

---

[1] Matthew Arnold.   [2] Chalmers.
          [3] "Guesses at Truth.'

cloak of it. But it is within our power to repair this cloak when it wears thin, by putting ourselves under the spell of those whose larger and stronger natures make them superior in this Christian grace.

One great means of doing this is to read the biographies of the saints, latter-day saints, many of them. Let us be careful in this branch of our reading, that we take the lives of *all* saints, not the saints of our own particular school, for so we shall learn also the other grace of sympathy. It is of the first importance to have firm convictions of our own, but it is of, at least, second importance to understand and sympathize with the convictions of others.

Not only does sympathy lead us to see the opinions of others in a truer light, it enables us to form a sounder judgment on our own; for as long as a man looks only "on his own things," he fails to see them in true proportion.

We shall surely rise above party spirit and narrowness, if we read with generous sympathy such books as Stanley's "Life of Arnold;" the lives of "Kingsley," "F. D. Maurice," "St. Catharine of Sienna" (by Mrs. Butler); "Mrs. Fry," "William Wilberforce," "Angélique Arnauld" (by Miss Martin); "St. Theresa" (by Miss Trench; also by Mrs. Cunningham Graham); "Charles Lowder," "Sir Henry Lawrence," and of "Lord Lawrence" (by Mr. Bosworth Smith); "John

Woolner the Quaker;" "The Hermits" (by Kingsley); "Disciples of St. John" (by Miss Yonge); "Letters of Edward Denison;" "St. Francis of Assisi" and "Edward Irving" (both by Mrs. Oliphant); "St. Vincent de Paul;" Walton's "Lives."

No suggestions on Sunday reading can fail to mention those "Companions of the Devout Life," treated in a volume of that name, which is itself fascinating Sunday reading. I mean the great devotional books of the world—"The Confessions of St. Augustine," "The Pilgrim's Progress," "Pensées de Pascal," "The Imitation," and "The Christian Year,"—books of the inner life of the best men of all ages, which teach us more than anything else can do, the essential oneness in spirit of all true lovers of God.

" I accept and believe," said Mr. Bright in one of his speeches many years ago, "in a very grand passage I once met with in the writings of the Founder of the State of Pennsylvania. He says that humble, meek, merciful, just, pious, and devout souls are everywhere of one religion, and when death has taken off the mask, they all know one another, though the divers liveries they wear here make them strangers."

Missionary work is surely one of the branches of Sunday study incumbent on us. Very likely you will say you do not care about it ; but this state of mind by no means absolves you from the duty of missionary work, and the prelude to that work is to learn something about it.

I grant that most missionary reports are dull when seen in the setting of our own general ignorance. But let us take one centre of missionary work, and make it a centre for our general reading. Read the best book of travels describing that country, read about its native religion, and the lives of its chief missionaries, and chief heroes (whether missionary or not). After this preparation we shall, for the future, read the missionary report with quite different eyes.

A few volumes of sermons would be a good element in our Sunday library.

Perhaps you may think that to hear sermons on Sunday is enough without reading any. But when we consider what a storehouse of instruction and devotion is contained in such books as the University Sermons of Dr. Newman, Dean Church, and Dr. Mozley, we must surely feel that they would widen and strengthen our spiritual life.

An invalid once gave me a list of sermons which she found specially helpful [1] (one for each day of the month), all taken from seven volumes that contain the essence of the Church of Bishop Andrewes and Bishop Butler :—Dean Church's " University Sermons," and " Pascal ; " Mozley's " University " and " Parochial " sermons ; Dean

[1] Page 231.

P

Paget's "Spirit of Discipline," and "Studies in the Christian Character;" and vol. i. of Newman's "Parochial Sermons." It is interesting to notice in connection with this last a passage in Isaac William's autobiography: "Newman had a peculiar power of seizing intellectually the ἦθος and principles of another, and making them his own, as it were on trial. I was struck with this afterwards in a remarkable manner, by the way in which he learned through me the γνῶμαι, as he called them, of Thomas Keble of Bisley, his character and principles; so that, at one time, when I walked daily with him, and we conversed on these subjects, I found the same views, drawn out and expressed in his own way, in his sermon at St. Mary's on the following Sunday. The first volume that he published is almost entirely made up of these, and will be found to differ on this account from his succeeding volumes as more practical. It has this marked distinguishable character, owing to this circumstance, and I always looked upon that volume as Bisley, passing through me, and appearing, developed by Newman, in St. Mary's pulpit."

There is one sermon I should like to add to the list, and that is Bishop Butler's sermon on the government of the tongue, which might be learnt by heart, instead of being merely read once a month.

A daily sermon will probably be more than you

require, but you may find the idea helpful of having a carefully chosen set of sermons, and reading them through several times, instead of going on to fresh ones.

When you read them the first time, mark the bits that go home to you and look on them as tuning-forks by which to set the pitch of your life. When you read them the second time, these marked bits will be so many questions in your self-examination as to how you have spent the time, since that special aspect of duty was brought to your notice.

Dr. Liddon says: " Especially should an effort be made on every Sunday in the year, to learn some portion of the Will of God more perfectly than before ; some truth or aspect of His Revelation of Himself in the gospel; some Christian duty, as taught by the example or the words of Christ. Without a positive effort of this kind a Sunday is a lost Sunday : we shall think of it thus in eternity." We probably all feel we need this strenuous mental effort of which Dr. Liddon speaks.

Is our religious knowledge any more exact and deep than it used to be (or at all events, has it improved in proper proportion to the years which have elapsed)—are we more able to give a reason for the faith that is in us ? We know our favourite author pretty well by this time—*e.g.* some of us could find most quotations from Browning or Tennyson, and if we come on a passage in them we do not understand, we work at it till we *do* understand. Have we improved in Bible knowledge?—beyond the formal reading of chapter after chapter, in the course of which, unless we had put a mark, we should sometimes find it hard to know where we left off!

The Theological School is open to women at Oxford, and it may surely be hoped that women will devote as much brain power to this as they do to History and Classics and Mathematics. These latter " schools " seem to us worthy of our best intellect, whereas in Bible study we are too often content with the baby-knowledge which we gained when we were small.

We must all acknowledge that women and girls, as a rule, have very scanty religious knowledge, and, only too often, unsettled views. Our religious education has not kept pace with our higher education. Perhaps the main cause is, that the conscience of women is not awake on the matter of solid religious instruction. If women had, as a body, realized that their intellects had a duty in the matter, as clearly as they do realize that their emotions have, the difficulty would be in a fair way of being met. Their conscience is awake on the subject of good little books, and these are read assiduously; but the ordinary girl of to-day is not so likely to realize this intellectual duty as was her grandmother. The Evangelical revival, though it did untold good spiritually, yet had the defect of its quality, and was apt to substitute emotional spiritual edification for instruction. The " Catholic " revival has also a share in causing the present deficiency, for it has led the younger generation towards attractive services, and has left no time on Sunday for the solid, instructive, "Sunday books " so profitably read by our grandmothers.

Much stress is laid in the present day, and quite rightly, on meditation. But in order to meditate profitably, we need something more than our own crude thoughts. If even St. Paul sent for his "books and parchments," can we afford to dispense with such assistance as can be derived from the study of higher and holier minds than our own ?

As women (whether professional teachers or not) we shall each have to teach and guide some one in religious matters. We ought to have a general grasp of the subject for this purpose, besides the personal help of knowing our Bibles thoroughly.

As regards reading theology to settle one's own mind, I am not sure that arguments do much good. I fancy Doubt is one of the evil spirits which goeth not out but by prayer and fasting.

You may say that I do not allow due weight to the *intellectual* difficulties which beset Christianity. Perhaps so, for, personally, I see no other practical and practicable clue to life but the Lord Jesus Christ. I can quite understand that arguments are needed by a more logical mind, but as far as *argument* goes, it seems to me that the negation of Christianity is beset by more difficulties still.[1] Most of the difficulties connected with Christianity are difficulties common to every thoughtful mind, whether Christian or not; problems which are inherent in life, and which it is unfair to charge to Christianity as such.

There is a great deal of doubt flying about, some of it is a real trial allowed by God, some is fashion, some is laziness; for the non-Christian side comes before us without any trouble, in magazine articles, while the defence needs some study and trouble. I have never yet met a girl who complained of doubts and who had given so much as a year's hard study, under direction, to theology. I do not say the year would have answered her questions, but it would have been an earnest that she grudged no trouble, it would have been part of the 'fasting' and self-denial which *would* have helped.

Doubt is sometimes a wish to evade the tremendously high standard imposed by Christ, a standard which the last of Mr. Gore's " Bampton Lectures " helps us to realize.

Mrs. Hannah More said, of the people in her day who complained that the Athanasian Creed was a stumbling-block to them, that she always

[1] Cp. R. Browning, "Bishop Blougram's Apology," etc.

shrewdly suspected the real stumbling-block was the Ten Commandments ! A girl does not actually wish to break a commandment, but her conscience is more at ease when she is only balancing 'views' for and against Christianity, than when she is standing face to face with a real Master Who claims a part of her every thought and action.

Definite study is desirable because, though Doubt may not attack you personally, you may have to talk to those who suffer under it, and it is well to be able to detect the weak points in their chain of difficulties. Besides, a course of this reading is very useful in clearing the air, it makes you less likely to be attracted by suggestions from the other side, if you know that they are an old story, met and conquered long ago. I do not say that this is true of all suggested difficulties, by any means, though it is of many. The universe would be narrow indeed if our present brains could see the answer to everything !

Also, though arguments may not meet your special difficulties, yet a steady course of reading will help you. It clears up the mistiness of your mind; you do not find an answer to your special question, but your difficulties, generally, take truer proportions—*you* get clearer headed. I should say, do not read about your special question, attack your unsettledness indirectly. Forgive me for saying it, but girls are apt to be very muddle-headed, and I have read and listened to 'intellectual doubts,' in which the intellect appeared to be conspicuous by its absence! The only argument that seemed applicable was Cromwell's to his Parliament, 'I beseech you, my beloved brethren, I beseech you by the mercies of Christ, to believe that you may be mistaken.'

Most women would do well to recognize that these matters require real intellect and years of study, before one could venture to differ from the great minds who have studied the question and who have set to their seal that God is true.

You may say that many great and wise men have arrived at a different conclusion. True, but many of those are out of court in the question, because they did not try to find the 'doctrine' by doing 'the will,' but I will grant that some (many if you like) were Christlike, though they failed to find Christ. Well, then, if it is to be a question of authority, it seems wiser, all other things being equal, to pin one's faith to those who *did* find a clue to life. Of course I do not allow that all other things *are* equal, but even if I went so far as that, I should feel that Bishop Butler ("Analogy," II. vi.) left a very serious responsibility on us to act as if Christianity were true.

Let us suppose that a girl wishes to give her tithe of intellect as well as of other things to religion, how had she better do it? Many currents in the present tide of affairs distract the ordinary girl from religious study, and, if she yet wishes to improve herself, she is frightened by feeling the vastness of the subject. One book here, and one book there, seems such a drop in the ocean, and very likely she will find that she has read something as much out of date as if she studied Miss Martineau's stories for her political economy. She needs direction : who is to give it?

Women have now special facilities at Oxford for religious study, and I hope that some of the students who intend to be headmistresses, or special parish workers, may give an extra year to such work. But this will not solve the difficulty of religious education for the upper classes. The expense is too great and the work too hard, for ordinary cases. What can be suggested for the ordinary woman who has no special time, brains, or money at her disposal, and who yet wishes to be able to give a reason for the faith that is in her?

There are various branches of the subject, to each of which she owes some study—study of the Bible itself; the present position of science and of criticism with regard to religion; dogmatics; Church history; illustration of the Bible in modern discoveries and travel; practical devotional reading. Of those seven heads, I confidently affirm that the devotional reading is the only one in which the average woman could stand examination, and yet it is her duty to know something of the other six. How is she to be helped? I should like her to have definite guidance in religious study, by means of an authorized scheme of reading, giving under such headings as I named just now, the minimum course of reading[1] which an average woman should feel bound to master, as an elementary part of her education.

I should like to be able to say to a girl: Read this perfectly practicable list of books before you feel yourself capable of forming an opinion. I should like it to be recommended in school magazines, in " old girls' " reading societies; I should like to see a society among the staff of every school for reading it through together. The Divinity School offers a course too deep, and consequently too limited, to meet the needs of the average woman. The various diocesan schemes and the Sunday-school institutes issue something of the kind, but they involve several years' consecutive study, and many people would prefer a shorter scheme put forth as a whole, and not in parts. If it were issued as a penny leaflet (revised often enough to be kept up to date), it would be thankfully followed by many who would hesitate to enrol themselves as members of a diocesan scheme. There might be more than one such list, so as to give scope for varying views, but

[1] Suggested course, p. 222.

authorization by some committee of repute would be a strong feature of the desired usefulness.

A headmistress often recommends a book because it suits her personally, and it is read by the girl, who personally believes in her; but it would be very different if she could say that such and such a responsible body of clergy recommend this list as the minimum course of reading for every conscientious Churchwoman. I believe nine girls out of every ten, and teachers too, and Sunday-school teachers and district visitors, would gladly follow such a definite course. They cannot in this busy and migratory age feel sure of attending any set of lectures, or of keeping up year by year with any one diocesan reading scheme, but they would keep such a short list by them, and work their way through it in course of time. At present they are frightened by the width of the subject, or read a book here and a pamphlet there, as their various advisers suggest, never getting any general idea of the subject, such as they have of English literature or history. The very superficiality of such a list would have the quality of its defect, and would induce many to adopt it who would be afraid of a more lengthy and thorough scheme, though it would probably lead them on to the better work of the diocesan reading societies. I am not advocating superficiality as opposed to solid reading, but superficiality as opposed to the utter ignorance which now too often prevails.

Suppose such a scheme of reading were issued, and were recommended by clergy and teachers, would this be enough? No! The tendency of modern education is more in the direction of oral teaching than of private reading.

The clergy, being already overworked, can hardly attend to the religious education of all upper-class girls or women in the parish; it is hard work already to see to the poor, and it is seldom possible to make the Sunday afternoon catechizing profitable to both rich and poor. A thoughtful girl, accustomed to the hard head-work of good school methods, requires her teaching in divinity to be as intellectual as the rest of her school work. Such girls do desire help in this matter. If every clergyman would recommend such a list, or issue one himself, I am certain nine-tenths of the women and girls in his parish would read it if he definitely told them to do so. The Sunday-school catechizing does not help them; and the clergyman is too busy to hold a special class for them; but could he not organize such a class, where the outlines of the Faith could be studied, under some one of the clever unattached women to be found in most congregations? Such a woman would be glad of the intellectual scope this class would offer; she would have leisure to prepare for it ; and in time, when such a class should become a recognized part of the usual parochial machinery (as mothers' meetings are now), one might hope that such women would go to Oxford to prepare seriously for the work. The teaching could be kept under the clergyman's own hand, as much as in the Sunday school, and he would find such a class a great help in doing for him the more formal part of his confirmation work, and leaving him more time for the spiritual part.

With older girls it would be a nursery of parish workers, where they could be trained and tested before being turned loose in a Sunday school, just because *here* is a class and *there* is a young lady, and it seems natural to put the two together, without in the least knowing what the combination will produce.

These are small remedies—advice in reading and upper-class Bible lessons. Doubtless, they are already at work in many places, but they are not as yet part of the ordinary machinery of every parish. It might seem more to the purpose to urge something new, *e.g.* the Oxford Divinity School, now open to women ; but religious education amongst women is at such a low ebb, that a small remedy may be more efficacious as a beginning. Every day one sees more clearly the danger of leaving women as untaught as they now undoubtedly are, in spite of the opportunities for learning which surround

them. Women do not like religious *study*, though
they enjoy religious *reading*, but they would carry
out a short scheme if their own clergyman told
them to do it; and though it would not meet
all the difficulties of the day, it would obviate
what makes nine-tenths of the *danger* of those
difficulties, *i.e.* the mistiness and emptiness of their
own minds on this matter. Women have developed
their minds in nearly all other subjects, but in
religion they are content with the baby-knowledge
of the nursery.

In that severely helpful book, Law's "Serious
Call," there is a striking picture of the man whose
powers and brain and knowledge were deepened
and cultivated by every year of his life, but whose
prayers remain as elementary as when he was a
child. Is not the same thing but too often true
of women,—not of their prayers, perhaps, but of
their religious knowledge?

SUNDAY READING.

A.—A MINIMUM COURSE OF READING FOR AN AVERAGE WOMAN.

Jewish Church. 3 vols. *A. P. Stanley.* 6s. each.
Life of the Messiah. 2 vols. *Dr. Edersheim.* 24s. or 7s. 6d.
Life and Epistles of S. Paul. *Conybeare and Howson.*
  3s. 6d.

Illustrations of the Creed. *Elizabeth Wordsworth.* 5*s.*
Some Elements of Religion. *H. P. Liddon.* 1*s.* 6*d.*
Primer of Biblical Geography. *Lieut. Conder.* 3*s.* 6*d.*
History of Religion in England. *H. O. Wakeman.* 1*s.* 6*d.*

SPECIAL BOOKS ON THEOLOGY.

Bampton Lectures on the Incarnation. *C. Gore.* 7*s.* 6*d.*
The Atonement. *R. W. Dale.* 4*s.* *net.*
The Resurrection. *W. Milligan.* 5*s.*
The Ascension. *W. Milligan.* 7*s.* 6*d.*

B.—BOOKS FOR FURTHER STUDY.[1]

GENERAL BOOKS ON THE OLD TESTAMENT.

*Discipline of the Christian Character. *R. W. Church.* 4*s.* 6*d.*
Doctrine of the Prophets. *A. F. Kirkpatrick.* 6*s.*
*Prophets and Kings. *F. D. Maurice.* 3*s.* 6*d.*
*Patriarchs and Law-givers. *F. D. Maurice.* 3*s.* 6*d.*
*Sermons on the Old Testament. *H. P. Liddon.* 5*s.*
Early Religion of Israel. *Robertson.* 10*s.* 6*d.*
*Jewish Church. 3 vols. *A. P. Stanley.* 6*s.* *each.*
*Divine Library of the Old Testament. *A. F. Kirkpatrick.*
  3*s.* *net.*
The Canon of the Old Testament. *H. Ryle.* 6*s.*
Ruling Ideas of Early Ages. *J. B. Mozley.* 6*s.*
*Guild Manual. *Robertson.* 6*d.*
*The Temple and its Services. *Dr. Edersheim.* 3*s.* 6*d.*

---

[1] This list is more exhaustive than is necessary for general reading, but it was compiled by the help of such valuable advice that it is thought better to print it in full. An asterisk is prefixed to the easier books.

Special Books of the Old Testament.

*Notes on Genesis. *F. W. Robertson.* 3s. 6d.

*Early Narratives of Genesis. *H. Ryle.* 3s. net.

*The Book Genesis, a true History. *Watson.* 2s.

After the Exile. 2 vols. *Hunter.* 5s. each.

Lectures on the Book of Job. *Bradley.* 7s. 6d.

The Psalms. Book I. *A. F. Kirkpatrick.* 3s. 6d.

Psalm Mosaics. *A. S. Dyer.* 7s. 6d.

The Book of Psalms (abridged ed.). *Bp. Perowne.* 10s. 6d.

      ,,   ,,   translated by *Prof. Cheyne.* 6s.

Lectures on Ecclesiastes. *Bradley.* 4s. 6d.

Isaiah (Expositor's Bible). 2 vols. *G. A. Smith.* 7s. 6d.

The Story of Daniel. *Hunter.* 5s.

The Minor Prophets. *E. B. Pusey.* 31s. 6d.

*The Minor Prophets (Expositor's Bible). *G. A. Smith.*
    7s. 6d.

Dictionary of the Bible. 4 vols. *Smith.* £4 4s.

*Cambridge Bible Series. About 3s. 6d. each.

*Difficulties of the Old Testament. *H. Winnington Ingram.*
    6d.

General Books on the New Testament.

*Life of the Messiah. *Dr. Edersheim.* 24s. or 7s. 6d.

Introduction to the New Testament. *G. Salmon.* 9s.

*Pastor Pastorum. *Latham.* 6s. 6d.

*Notes on the Parables. *R. C. Trench.* 7s. 6d.

*Studies in the Gospels. *R. C. Trench.* 10s. 6d.

Synonyms of the New Testament. *R. C. Trench.* 12s.

*Harmony. *Fuller.* (*S.P.C.K.*) 1s. 6d.

Introduction to Study of the Gospels. *Bp. Westcott.* 10s. 6d.

Life of our Lord (Hulsean Lectures). *Bp. Ellicott.* 12s.

Life of Christ. *Jeremy Taylor.* s. h.

Origin of Christianity. *Fisher.* 12s. 6d.

*Difficulties of the New Testament. *H. Winnington Ingram.*
    6d.

Special Books on the New Testament.

*Commentary on the Gospels. *S.P.C.K.* 7s. 6d.

*Key to the Gospels. *T. P. Norris.* 1s. 6d.

*Footprints of the Son of Man. (S. Mark.) *H. M. Luckock.* 3s. 6d.

Gospel according to S. John. *Bp. Westcott.* 10s. 6d.

*Creed and Character. (S. John's Gospel.) *H. S. Holland.* 3s. 6d.

The Great 40 Days. *Bp. Moberly.* 5s.

S. Paul as Traveller and Roman Citizen. *Ramsay.* 12s. 6d.

*God's City. (Acts.) *H. S. Holland.* 3s. 6d.

*Key to the Acts. *J. P. Norris.* 2s. 6d.

First Age of the Church. *Döllinger.* s.h.

Church in the Roman Empire. *Ramsay.* 12s.

*Life and Epistles of S. Paul. *Conybeare and Howson.* 3s. 6d.

Dissertations on the Apostolic Age. *Bp. Lightfoot.* 14s.

Epistle to the Romans. *H. P. Liddon.* 14s.

Epistle to the Romans (Speaker's Commentary). *Gifford.* 7s. 6d.

Biblical Essays. *Bp. Lightfoot.* 12s.

*Lectures on the Corinthians. *F. W. Robertson.* 5s.

Galatians (Expositor's Bible). *Findlay.* 7s. 6d.

Epistle to the Ephesians. *R. W. Dale.* 7s. 6d.

Christus Consummator. (Hebrews.) *Westcott.* 6s.

The Jewish Temple and the Christian Church. *R. W. Dale.* 7s. 6d.

Book of Revelation. *W. Milligan.* 7s. 6d.

Theology.

Faith of the Gospels. *A. Mason.* 3s. 6d.

*Rudiments of Theology. *J. P. Norris.* 3s. 6d.

Lectures on Religion. *Leighton Pullan.* 6s.

Historic Faith. *Bp. Westcott.* 6s.

Foundations of the Creed. *Bp. Hervey Goodwin.* 14*s.*
*Introduction to the Creed. *Maclear.* 2*s.* 6*d.*
Sermons of S. Leo. *W. Bright.* 4*s.* 6*d.*
Manual of Theology. *Strong.* 5*s.*
Nicene Creed. *Forbes.* 6*s.*
*Illustrations of the Creed. *Elizabeth Wordsworth.* 5*s.*
Lux Mundi. 7*s.* 6*d.*
Theism. *Flint.* 7*s.* 6*d.*

Or

The Grounds of Theistic and Christian Belief. *Fisher.*
10*s.* 6*d.*
Chief End of Revelation. *Bruce.* 6*s.*
Reasonable Apprehensions and Reassuring Hints. *Footman.*
2*s.* 6*d.*

Special Subjects.

The Incarnation.
  Bampton Lectures. *H. P. Liddon.* 5*s.*
    ,,   ,,   *C. Gore.* 7*s.* 6*d.*
  The Incarnation. *R. Wilberforce.* 7*s.* 6*d.*
  De Incarnatione, trans. by Robertson. *S. Athanasius.*
  3*s.*

The Atonement.
  The Atonement. *R. W. Dale.* 4*s. net.*
  Cur Deus Homo (Translation). *S. Anselm.* 1*s.*

The Resurrection.
  The Gospel of the Resurrection. *Bp. Westcott.* 6*s.*
  The Resurrection. *W. Milligan.* 5*s.*

The Ascension.
  The Ascension. *W. Milligan.* 7*s.* 6*d.*

The Holy Spirit.
  Bampton Lectures. *Bp. Moberly.* 7*s.* 6*d.*
  *The Holy Spirit. *Bp. Webb.* 3*s.* 6*d.*

Miracles.

Bampton Lectures. *T. Mozley.* 3s. 6d.
*Notes on the Miracles. *R. C. Trench.* 7s. 6d.
Miracles. *Cox.* 2s. 6d.

CRITICISM AND THE BIBLE.

The Bible in the Church. *Bp. Westcott.* 4s. 6d.
Biblical Study. *Briggs.* 7s. 6d.
*Christus Comprobator. *Bp. Ellicott.* 2s.
The Oracles of God. *W. Sanday.* 4s.
Inspiration (Bampton Lectures). *W. Sanday.* 7s. 6d.

SCIENCE AND THE BIBLE.

Relations between Religion and Science (Bampton Lectures).
Bp. Temple. 6s.
Science and the Faith. *Aubrey Moore.* 3s. 6d.
Evolution and Religious Thought. *Le Conte.* 6s.
Christianity in Relation to Science and Morals. *MacColl.*
6s.
Does Science aid Faith? *Cotterill.* 3s. 6d.
Apologetics. Part I. *Bruce.* 10s. 6d.

ILLUSTRATIONS OF THE BIBLE.

*Helps to the Study of the Bible (Oxford). 1s. or 4s. 6d.
*Companion to the Bible (Camb.). 1s. or 5s.
Historical Geography of the Holy Land. *G. A. Smith.* 15s.
*Primer of Biblical Geography. *Conder.* 3s. 6d.
*Sinai and Palestine. *Stanley.* 12s.
*Fresh Light from Ancient Monuments. *Sayce.* 3s.
*Natural History of the Bible. *Tristram.* 5s.
*The Bible and the East. *Conder.* 5s.

CHURCH HISTORY.

History of the Church. *Schaff.* 42s.

Student's English Church History. *Perry.* 3 vols. 7*s.* 6*d.* each.

*History of Religion in England. *II. O. Wakeman.* 1*s.* 6*d.*

*History of the Church of England. *II. O. Wakeman.* 7*s.* 6*d.*

*Illustrated Notes on English Church History. *Lane.* 2 vols. 1*s.* each.

*'Turning Points of English Church History. *Cutts.* 3*s.* 6*d.*

*A Key to Church History. Ancient, and Modern. *Blunt.* 2*s.* 6*d.* each.

Early.

*Creed and Character. *H. S. Holland.* 3*s.* 6*d.*

Ecclesiastical History (Translated). *Eusebius.* 5*s.*

History of the Church, A.D. 313-451. *Bright.* 10*s.* 6*d.*

Church History. Vol. I. *Bp. Wordsworth.* 8*s.* 6*d.*

    ,,   ,,   Vols. II., III., and IV. 6*s.* each.

Christian Church during First Six Centuries. *Cheetham.* 10*s.* 6*d.*

Early Christianity. *Milman.* 3 vols. 4*s.* each.

*Eastern Church. *Stanley.* 6*s.*

Literary History of Christianity. *Cruttwell.* 2 vols. 21*s.*

Early English Church History. *Bright.* 12*s.*

*Waymarks in Church History. *Bright.* 7*s.* 6*d.*

On the Church. *Palmer. s. h.*

Middle Ages.

Latin Christianity. *Milman.* 9 vols. 4*s.* each.

The Dark Ages. *Maitland.* 12*s. net.*

History of the Popes. *Ranke.* 3 vols. 3*s.* 6*d.* each.

History of the Papacy during the Reformation. *Bp Creighton.* Vols. I.-V. 3*s.* 6*d.* each.

*Lectures on Medieval Church History. *R. C. Trench.* 12*s.*

Middle Ages. *Hardwick.* 10*s.* 6*d.*

Reformation. *Hardwick.* 10*s.* 6*d.*

The English Church in the Middle Ages. *Hunt.* 2*s.* 6*d.*

History of the Church of England, 1529-1558. *Dixon.*
4 vols. 16*s. each.*
Lectures on the Reformation. *Aubrey Moore.* 16*s.*
Reformation in England. *Perry.* 2*s.* 6*d.*
*The Church and the Puritans. *H. O. Wakeman.* 2*s.* 6*d.*
Lectures on the Reformation. *Beard.* 4*s.* 6*d.*

Special Books.

*The Church and the Roman Empire. *Carr.* 2*s.* 6*d.*
*The Church of the Early Fathers. *Plummer.* 2*s.* 6*d.*
*Three Great Fathers. *Bright.* 6*s.*
*The Fathers for English Readers:—Ambrose, Basil,
Jerome, Augustine, Leo, Gregory, Synesius. 2*s. each.*
(*S.P.C.K.*)
Life and Times of S. Chrysostom. *Stephens.* 7*s.* 6*d.*
*The Arian Controversy. *H. N. Gwatkin.* 2*s.* 6*d.*
Conversion of the West. *Maclear.* 4 vols. 2*s. each.*
Leaders of the Northern Church. *Bp. Lightfoot.* 6*s.*
*Venerable Bede. *Browne.* 2*s.*
*Alfred the Great. *Hughes.* 6*s.*
*S. Anselm. *R. W. Church.* 5*s.*
*Wycliffe and Early Movements of Reform. *Lane Poole.*
2*s.* 6*d.*
Wycliffe and his English Precursors. *Lechler.* 8*s.*
Oxford Reformers. *Seebohm.* 14*s.*

SERMONS, ETC.

Hall's Contemplations. *s. h.*
Leighton on S. Peter. *s. h.*
Jeremy Taylor's Sermons. *s. h.*
Butler's Analogy. Edited by *W. E. Gladstone.* 10*s.*
  ,,   Sermons.   ,,   ,,   10*s.*
Law's Serious Call. 1*s*
  ,, Letters. *s. h.*
  ,, Treatise on Christian Perfection. *s. h.*

*Goulburn's Thoughts on Personal Religion. 3*s*. 6*d*.
*   ,,   Study of the Holy Scriptures. 2*s*. 6*d*.
Elements of Religion. *Liddon.* 2*s*. 6*d*.
*Discipline of the Christian Character. *R. W. Church.* 4*s*. 6*d*.
Human Life and its Conditions.   ,,   ,,   6*s*. 0*d*.
*Village Sermons.   ,,   ,,   6*s*. 0*d*.
Advent Sermons.   ,,   ,,   4*s*. 6*d*.
The Gifts of Civilization.   ,,   ,,   7*s*. 6*d*.
*The Hallowing of Work. *F. Paget.* 2*s*.
*Faculties and Difficulties of Belief and Disbelief. *F. Paget.*
    6*s*. 6*d*.
Studies in the Christian Character. *F. Paget.* 4*s*. 6*d*.
*Sermon on the Mount. *C. Gore.* 3*s*. 6*d*.
University Sermons. *Illingworth.* 5*s*.
Personality Human and Divine. *Illingworth.* 8*s*. 6*d*.
*Advent to Lent. *Aubrey Moore.* 3*s*. 6*d*.
The Decalogue. *Elizabeth Wordsworth.* 4*s*. 6*d*.
*The Revelation of the Risen Lord. *Bp. Westcott.* 6*s*.
Prophets and Kings. *F. D. Maurice.* 3*s*. 6*d*.
*Sermons. *F. W. Robertson.* 3*s*. 6*d*. *each vol.*
The Lord's Prayer. *Elizabeth Wordsworth.* 4*s*. 6*d*.
*The Candle of the Lord. *Phillips Brooks.* 6*s*.
Lectures on Preaching. *R. W. Dale.* 6*s*.
Laws of Christ for Common Life. *R. W. Dale.* 6*s*.
Hours of Thought. *J. Martineau.* 7*s*. 6*d*.
Endeavours after the Christian Life. *J. Martineau.* 7*s*. 6*d*.

DEVOTIONAL BOOKS.

The Imitation of Christ.
Spiritual Letters. *S. Francis de Sales.* 2*s*. 6*d*.
Spiritual Letters to Men. *Fénélon.* 2*s*. 6*d*.
Spiritual Letters to Women. *Fénélon.* 2*s*. 6*d*.
Avis Spirituels. 2*s*. 6*d*.
Brief Thoughts and Meditations. *R. C. Trench.*

Thoughts on the Christian Life. *H. Bowman.* 1*s.* 6*d.*
Instructions in the Devout Life. *Bp. Wilkinson.* 6*d.*
Hints on Meditation. *W. Trevelyan.* 2*d.*
The Still Hour. *J. Stalker.* 1*d.*

PRAYERS.

The Book of Private Prayer (issued by Convocation). 2*s.*
Sacra Privata. *Bp. Wilson.* 1*s.*
Bishop Andrewes' Devotions. 1*s.*
The Armoury of Prayer. *Berdmore Compton.* 3*s.* 6*d.*
Before the Throne. *Bellairs.* 2*s.* 6*d.*
Private Prayers. *E. B. Pusey.* 1*s.*
The Golden Grove. *Jeremy Taylor.* 1*s.* 6*d.*

A MONTH'S SERMONS.[1]

PAROCHIAL SERMONS. Vol. I. *J. H. Newman.*
Secret Faults.
Religious Use of Excited Feeling.
Times of Private Prayer.
Forms of Private Prayer.
Promising without Doing.
Self-denial the Test of Religious Earnestness.

UNIVERSITY SERMONS. *J. B. Mozley.*
The Peaceful Temper.
The Reversal of Human Judgment.
The Strength of Wishes.
Our Duty to our Equals.

PAROCHIAL SERMONS. *J. B. Mozley.*
Influences of Habit on Devotion.
The Life of Probation.
Thought for To-morrow.
Growing Worse.
The Educating Power of Strong Impressions.

[1] Page 209.

UNIVERSITY SERMONS. *R. W. Church.*
Human Judgment and Divine Temper.
Self-Discipline.
The Sense of Beauty.
The Power of the Ascension.

PASCAL AND OTHER SERMONS. *R. W. Church.*
Particular Providence.
Strong Words.

THE SPIRIT OF DISCIPLINE. *F. Paget.*
The Sorrow of the World.
The Perils of the Vacant Heart.
Leisure Thoughts.

STUDIES IN THE CHRISTIAN CHARACTER. *F. Paget.*
Honouring all Men.
Sanity of Saintliness.
Forbearance.
Courtesy.
Misuse of Words.
Cowardice.
Simplicity of Goodness.

ON THE PRAYER BOOK.

History of the Book of Common Prayer. *Proctor.* 10s. 6d.
Annotated Book of Common Prayer. *J. H. Blunt.* 21s.
Principles of Divine Service. *Archdeacon Freeman.* s. h.
Studies in the History of the Prayer Book. *H. M. Luckock.* 6s.
The Divine Liturgy. *H. M. Luckock.* 6s.
Voices of the Prayer Book. *W. C. E. Newbolt.* 2s. 6d.
Preparation of Prayer Book Lessons. *C. M. Yonge.* 6s.
Conversations on the Catechism. *C. M. Yonge.* s. h.

" The Pilgrim's Progress."

DR. JOHNSON once took Bishop Percy's little girl on his knee and asked her if she had read "The Pilgrim's Progress." "No," said the child. "Then you are not worth a farthing," exclaimed the doctor, as he put her down.

One hopes that she went forthwith and read it, for a child's mental landscape is much impoverished if it lacks the wicket gate and the House Beautiful, if she never hears the birds singing the Old Hundredth in the trees of the Land of Beulah, and never overhears Giant Despair's consultations with his wife. But it is not the obvious charm of the vivid pictures and forcible language, on which I would dwell here, but the value of the book as part of our Devotional Library.

Let no one object to "The Pilgrim's Progress," as being childish, or for unlettered people, since Coleridge said every man should read it three times, as a poet, as a theologian, and as a Christian.

"How much the world owes to great sorrows!"[1]

[1] Prof. Seeley.

Had Bunyan never " lighted on a certain place where was a den," what blanks there would be in our spiritual maps ! The geography of Europe may be altered by wars and rumours of wars without its making much difference to many of us, but Doubting Castle, the Slough of Despond, the Valley of the Shadow of Death, Vanity Fair, the Land of Beulah, and the Delectable Mountains are more than mere geographical expressions to us ; they have given a local habitation and a name to many a painful conflict, many a vision of the Celestial City, which come to the pilgrim of to-day, as surely as to Bunyan in his " den." For us, also, " The House Beautiful stands by the wayside ; " for us, also, " Giant Despair sometimes falls into fits in sunshiny weather." We, also, should say, as did the pilgrims one to another, " We have need to cry to the Strong for strength," and should heed the Shepherd's rejoinder, " Ay, and you will have need to use it too, when you have it." We, too, can be like Christian, glad and lightsome, and say with a merry heart, " He hath given me rest by his sorrow, and life by His death." We, too, have " to play the man in Vanity Fair," and need to say to ourselves, " To go back is nothing but death : to go forward is fear of death, and life everlasting beyond it : I will yet go forward :" or, at least, to say with Mr. Feeblemind, " Brunts I look for, but this I have resolved on, to wit, to run where I can,

to go where I cannot run, and to creep where I
cannot go."

Is there any other book which has thus enriched
our mental picture gallery with scenes, so real and
sacred, that they form a continuous series in our
minds with those of Bible history? Are not
Christian and Greatheart as real to us as any
heroes of Hebrew history? Do not Bunyan and
Milton monopolize the honour of having modified
popular theology, and given shape and vividness
to many ideas, which, though implied in the Bible,
would be overlooked, but for " Paradise Lost " and
" The Pilgrim's Progress " ? How peopled must
the Bedford prison have been with these creations,
whose circumstances and relationships were so real
to Bunyan! Who has not felt the delight of over-
hearing the private talk of a real giant with his
wife? Who has not felt he has often been past
the place " where they saw one Fool, and one
Want-wit, washing of an Ethiopian, with intention
to make him white " ? Who has not felt the
satisfactoriness of knowing about Mr. Hold-the-
World, Mr. Money-love, and Mr. Save-all, with a
fulness of detail that made them seem next-door
neighbours ; how, in " their minority they were
schoolfellows and taught by one Mr. Gripeman, a
schoolmaster in Love-gain, which is a market town
in the County of Coveting, in the North ? " Who
has not delighted in the family history of By-ends,

who had so many good connections, but " in especial my Lord Turn-about, my Lord Time-server, my Lord Fair-speech; also Mr. Smoothman, Mr. Facing-both-ways, Mr. Anything; while the parson of the parish, Mr. Two-tongues, was his mother's own brother, by the father's side, so that he was a gentleman of good quality, though his great-grandfather was but a waterman, looking one way and rowing another."

A clergyman once told me that he had found it a most helpful means of Bible study to read " The Pilgrim's Progress," finding all the references. He said that, until he did this, he had had no idea what a fresh light Bunyan threw on many passages of scripture, by his use of them, and by the manner in which he connected one with another. It has often seemed to me a pity that this book is not used as a basis for lessons; a series might be drawn out which could be used, instead of stories, at afternoon Sunday school, and which would give vividness to many children's ideas of the Christian's journey.

Bunyan is a writer who has a special message to us in the present day, when, owing to a natural reaction from Puritanism, the sense of sin is seldom dwelt upon. Exhortations to philanthropy are sure to be heard and read, and ideals of moral excellence are plentiful; but Dean Stanley has had a large share in moulding this generation, and

Dr. Pusey has remarked how, in him, the sense of sin was curiously absent.

" 'The Pilgrim's Progress' " " plays upon the bass," and its story pleases the young better than does its underlying meaning. But its beauty and nobleness delight all readers, and the days will come when " the still sad music " which underlies that beauty will be welcomed for its own sake, and will bring double comfort for being an old friend.

To us, as to Christian, there comes in our dark hours " a man whose name is Help," and it is Bunyan himself, who brings us " the comfort wherewith he himself was comforted of God." We feel the inward gravity of Bunyan's own soul speaking to us, as we hear Christian telling Apollyon that " as for present deliverances he does not much expect it."

" No one can tell what in that combat attends us but he that hath been in the battle himself," and we feel the living grasp of Bunyan's own hand, as we take heart in hearing Christian's answer to the warnings of Mr. Worldly Wiseman : " Thou art likely to meet with wearisomeness, painfulness, hunger, perils, nakedness, sword, lions, dragons, darkness, and, in a word, death, and what not !"

" Why, sir," says Christian, " this burden upon my back is more terrible to me than are all these things which you have mentioned ; nay, methinks I care not what things I meet with in the way, if so be I can also meet with deliverance from my burden."

To Christian (as to Valiant, long afterwards), "these things seemed but as so many nothings," for he had seen his Lord "upon a mercy-seat, where He sits all the year long, to give pardon and forgiveness to them that come. . . . He longed to do something for the honour and glory of the Name of the Lord Jesus; yea, he thought that, had he a thousand gallons of blood in his body, he could spill it all for the sake of the Lord Jesus. . . . Things were right betwixt the Prince of Pilgrims and his soul." The " thought of what waited for him on the other side, lay as a glowing coal at his heart." And yet we are made to feel, over and over again, that "*burthened* Christian" is the true description of him. When Prudence asks, "Do you not find sometimes as if those things were vanquished, which at other times are your perplexity?" he answers, "Yes, but that is but seldom; but they are to me golden hours in which such things happen to me."

Our education generally takes us to the House Beautiful, though we sometimes "go past it unheeding;" sometimes because our hearts are so full of some Hill Difficulty we have been climbing, or of the lions in the way, or simply because we are in a hurry. As a rule, however, we do learn to be appreciative of beauty, and we visit with keen

interest the Interpreter's House; but we are in-
creasingly apt to miss out, on our journey, the Valley
of Humiliation, and the Valley of the Shadow,
"which was a very solitary place." Hence our
mental faculties are developed in modern life, more
than is the case with our moral thoughtfulness.
It is to our own most grievous loss, both of
pleasure and profit, when our life is so full of "the
blessed (?) influence of high pressure" if we
miss the valley, where "our Lord formerly had
His country house, and loved much to be," and
where the shepherd boy dwelt with "the herb
called heartsease in his bosom," and where "a
man shall be free from the noise and hurryings of
this life," so that some have wished that "the next
way to their Father's house were here, so that they
might be troubled no more with either hills or
mountains to go over."

This valley is "as fruitful a place as any the crow
flies over—there is no rattling with coaches, nor
rumbling with wheels; methinks, here one may,
without much molestation, be thinking what he is,
whence he came, what he has done, and to what
the King has called him." It is often in our own
power to save time (!) by avoiding this valley; but
if we do, the unavoidable passage through Vanity
Fair is made trebly dangerous; for Vanity Fair is
no longer a place of open peril, as it was to Christian and Faithful (which was in itself a warning),

it is more often, as Mnason described it, " full
of hurry in fair-time ; "—I had almost written
" term "-time ! " It is hard keeping our hearts and
spirits in any good order, when we are in a
cumbered condition. He that lives in such a place
as this is (Vanity Fair), and that has to do with
such as we have, has need of an item, to caution
him to take heed, every moment of the day."

Inward gravity of soul is the abiding temperament
of Bunyan's Christian,—

> " The gay at heart may wander to the skies,
>   And harps be found them, and a branch of palm
>   Be put into their hands," [1]

but Bunyan knows little of such ; he feels more at
home with one who knows what it is to have battles
with Apollyon " in a narrow place just beyond
Forgetful Green," or who feels conscious of belonging to the Town of Uncertain, or the Town of
Stupidity.   Bunyan is sensitive enough to know by
experience that it needs " a sunshine morning " for
Mr. Fearing to get over the Slough of Despond,
and that it helped him wonderfully when Evangelist
" gave him one smile."

We cannot doubt that Bunyan was a good
fighter, but he has curious sympathy with weak-
lings. Perhaps he had in him a touch of the
nature of Mr. Fearing, who carried a Slough of

[1] Quoted in " Friends in Council."

Despond in his mind (though he made nothing of
the lions); or it may have been sympathy with
Him Who loved pilgrims, that made Bunyan year
by year more tender to those "dejected at every
difficulty, who stumbled at every straw."   For this
compassionate insight grows in him,—it is only in
Part II. that we find those careful studies of
"desponds and slavish fears" which may make
the most cowardly reader say, with Christiana, "I
thought nobody had been like me, but this relation
of Mr. Fearing has done me good."

There are many books for the sick—"The
Pilgrim's Progress" is one for the dying also.
Except the Bible itself, where shall we find more
"comfortable words" for those on the brink of the
Dark River, than Christiana's cry, "Come wet, come
dry, I long to be gone; for, however the weather
is in my journey, I shall have time enough when I
come there to sit down and rest me and dry me."
Mr. Ready-to-halt lets us share the message that
came to him "in the Name of Him Whom he had
loved and followed, though upon crutches;" and
Mr. Stand-fast says to us, "This river has been a
terror to many; yea, the thoughts of it also have
often frightened me; yet the thoughts of what I
am going to, and of the conduct that waits for me
on the other side, doth lie as a glowing coal at my
heart.   I have loved to hear my Lord spoken of;
and wherever I have seen the print of His shoe

R

in the earth, there I have coveted to set my foot too. My toilsome days are ended. I shall be with Him in Whose company I delight myself."

But " The Pilgrim's Progress " is a book for the living—a manual for the pilgrim on his way to Jerusalem. Few of us are fortunate enough to dwell always " out of the reach of Giant Despair, where they can not so much as see Doubting Castle ; " and we may often be grateful for Christian's reminder that we " have in our bosoms a key called Promise, which will open any lock in Doubting Castle," and for Mr. Feeblemind's words, that he has " heard that not any pilgrim taken captive, if he keeps heartwhole towards his Master, is to die by the hand of the enemy." Hopeful's exhortations to pluck up heart should go home to us all, though it may be that some of us are like Mr. Fearing, who was " one that played upon the bass. He and his fellows sound the sackbut, whose notes are more doleful than the notes of other music are ; though, indeed, some say the bass is the ground of music. The first string that the musician touches is usually the bass, when he intends to put all in tune. God also plays upon this string first, when He sets the soul in tune for Himself. Only there was the imperfection of Mr. Fearing ; he could play on no other music than this."

But though Bunyan is " one of the Lord's

Shepherds indeed, who does not push the diseased aside, but rather strews their way into the palace with flowers," yet, the man who could condense twelve years of suffering and prison into the one line, " I lighted on a certain place where was a den," must have been Greatheart himself, who " loved greatly one that was a man of his hands." As Greatheart takes up Mr. Valiant's sword, surely it is the stout old Puritan of Bedford gaol who, when " he had looked there on a while, says, ' Ha ! it is a right Jerusalem blade !' "

www.ingramcontent.com/pod-product-compliance
Lightning Source LLC
Chambersburg PA
CBHW020057030726
47498CB00006B/1828